Mickey Mantle Day in Amsterdam

Another Novella
by Jim LaBate

Jim, I hope you enjoy this story about "the Mick"

Drawings by Brian Bateman

Published by

Mohawk River Press

Mohawk River Press
P.O. Box 4095
Clifton Park, New York 12065-0850
518-383-2254

Reprinted with permission: "Bobby Richardson's Homily for Mickey Mantle on August 15, 1995."

First Printing 1999
Printed in the United States of America

Library of Congress Catalog Card Number: 99-70005

ISBN 0-9662100-7-7

10 9 8 7 6 5 4 3 2 1

To Barbara — I love you, sweetheart.
You're even better than baseball.

Other works by Jim LaBate

Let's Go, Gaels — A Novella

Popeye Cantfield — A Full-Length Play

EAST
5S
NORTH
30
SOUTH
30

Chapter One

When most people think of Mickey Mantle Day, they think of June 8, 1969 — the day the Yankees retired his number seven in Yankee Stadium. I often think of that day myself. After all, my dad and I drove down the Thruway from Amsterdam and sat in the box seats right behind the Yankee dugout. But the only reason we had such good seats was because the Mick himself invited us and sent us free tickets. And the only reason he invited us was because he had such a good day in Amsterdam six years earlier. Here's what happened.

It was Wednesday, July 31, 1963. I was 12 years old, about to become a seventh grader at Saint Mary's Institute, and enjoying a summer full of baseball. I was in my third year of playing for Slezak's Gas Station in the Wee Men's League. During my first year, I played one half of an inning the entire year. I rode my bike to every game that year and then rode the bench while Kenny Kuk, Jimmy McMartin, Kurt Lallemand, Billy Whelly, and the Levandoski boys — Johnny and Billy — played all the time. Finally, during the last inning of the last game of the year, Coach Levandoski put me in. He told me to play center field, Mickey's position. We were playing at Isabel's Field that night, right next to the WCSS radio station, and I spent the whole half inning praying that nobody would hit the ball to me. I also prayed that the Knights of Columbus wouldn't score eight runs because if they did, I'd have to bat in the bottom of the sixth, and I wasn't ready for that yet. Fortunately, Billy Levandoski struck out the side with his big, sweeping, unhittable curve balls, and I survived my first game without any major embarrassment.

By the following summer, all the 12-year-olds from the year before had moved up to the Rookie League, and Coach Levandoski had decided I was ready to take Kenny Kuk's job at first base. I think he decided to put me there because I was the tallest kid on the team, and I'd have the best chance of catching all of Billy Whelly's high throws from shortstop. I did okay on defense, but I hit a miserable .114 for the year with five hits in 44 times up. And I had to get two hits in the last game to get my average up over .100.

1963, though, was different. I was having a great year. By the end of July, I was hitting .500: 15 hits in 30 trips to the plate. I had three doubles and a triple, too. The only thing I hadn't done was hit one over the wall, something that my best friend, Larry, teased me about all the time. Of course, he only had one home run himself, but that was a minor detail when it came to the baseball bragging rights of two 12-year-old hot shots.

So anyway, on this particular night, my dad and I were driving down Route 5-S toward Route 30. We had just come back from fixing a toilet at the house of one of Dad's bowling buddies up near the Auriesville Shrine. Dad worked as a plumber, and he was always getting calls during supper from friends and relatives to come over and take a look at a water heater or to unplug a backed-up toilet. During the school year, he always went by himself because Mom didn't want me out on school nights. But during the summer, he took me along with him, and I handed him tools while he worked, or I helped him clean up afterwards. Sometimes, his friends tried to slip me some money when we were done, but Dad never let me take any. And he never took any money for himself either. That's just the way he was.

So, by the time we finished that night, it was just starting to get dark. As we were getting close to the left turn for Route 30, we noticed a car on the shoulder of the road, with the hood up and a guy looking underneath. Naturally, Dad pulled over to see if he could help. He's never been as good at fixing cars as he is at fixing toilets or water heaters, but he was always willing to give it a shot.

When we drove by the car, parked, and started walking back toward it, I noticed the guy was huge and wore a nice pair of dress pants and a short-sleeve dress shirt. I figured he was a salesman of some kind. But when he turned from his car to face us, I couldn't believe my eyes. It was Mickey Mantle!

Dad didn't seem to notice at first, or, if he did, he was being real cool about it.

"Car died on ya, huh?" he said, and he shook hands with the greatest baseball player on the face of the earth.

I was speechless, but it didn't matter. They were too busy trying to figure out what was wrong with the car and what they could do to fix it.

"She was runnin' fine all day," Mickey said, "until the last mile or so. Then, she started wheezin' and coughin' and sputterin'. She sounded like Yogi Berra trying to score from second on a single," and he laughed at his own little joke, even though Yogi wasn't there to appreciate it.

Dad gave a second look at that point, and I still wasn't sure if he knew who he was helpin' or not. Dad has always been a St. Louis Cardinal fan, and he didn't watch much TV, so maybe he thought it was Stan Musial. I couldn't tell.

While they were workin', I walked back and looked in the windows of the car to see if Mickey had any balls or bats lying on the seats. He didn't. I saw a few candy-bar wrappers and an empty Coke bottle on the floor, but that was it. Then, Dad asked if he could try and start the car.

"Go ahead," Mickey said, and Dad climbed behind the wheel.

At that point, I was cut right in two. Part of me wanted the car to start immediately, so Mickey could see what a great mechanic my dad was. But the other part of me wanted the car to be dead, so we'd get to spend more time with Mickey. After all, if the car started and Mickey drove off, there's no way Larry and Bernie would ever believe that I met Mickey Mantle in person.

After thinking about all that, I said a little prayer, and the Lord answered it. The car didn't move or make a sound.

"We'll have to tow it for you," Dad said, as he got out of the car. "I got a chain right here in my trunk."

"Where we gonna tow it to?" Mickey asked.

"My buddy's got a gas station and repair place down in the East End. If it's okay with you, we'll tow it down there, and he can probably fix it up for ya first thing in the morning."

"That part sounds okay," Mickey said, "but is there a hotel nearby where I can spend the night?"

"You can stay at our house," I blurted out, my first words since we stopped.

Dad and Mickey both looked at me like I was a talking dog or something. Then, they laughed.

"Please?" I said to my dad. "He can sleep in my bed. I'll sleep on the floor. I'll sleep on the couch downstairs. I'll sleep on the back porch if I have to. Please let him stay, Dad. Please. Please. Please."

"I wouldn't want to be any trouble for y'all," Mickey said.

I couldn't tell if he was trying to be polite or if he didn't want to stay with us, so I kept talking.

"It wouldn't be any trouble; would it, Dad? We got plenty of room, plenty of food, and my sisters won't bother you at all. I'll make sure of that."

"It's okay with me," Dad said. "We'd be glad to put you up for the night."

"Please, Mr. Mantle?" I said in my best altar-boy manners. "I won't bother you either. I promise. Cross my heart and hope to die."

He looked at me real serious, like I'd just broken a picture window on his house, and he said: "Okay, I'll stay at your house, but you gotta promise me one thing."

"Anything, Mr. Mantle. I'll do anything."

"Don't call me 'Mr. Mantle.' My name's Mickey. And later I'll tell you the story behind that name."

"I know it already. I know the whole story. Your dad named you Mickey because —"

"Hold on there a minute, son," Mickey interrupted. "Your dad's doin' all the work, while you and I are blabberin' away."

Dad had pulled a chain out of the trunk and had put one end of the chain on our car and was getting set to put the other end on Mickey's car, so Mickey went to help. While they were attaching the chain, Mickey asked me, "What's your name?"

"My name's Jim," I said, "but my friends call me 'Jumbo.'"

"And later," my dad said to Mickey, "he'll tell you the story behind that name, too. And how you better not say 'Jumbo' in front of his mother."

"I promise," Mickey said, imitating me and laughing. "Cross my heart and hope to die."

"Okay, let's go," Dad said. "Is it all right if Jim rides with you?" he asked Mickey.

I couldn't believe it. I didn't even have to ask. I thought for sure Dad would make me ride with him, so he could tell me how to act and what to say and not say to Mickey.

"Hop in there, Jimbo," Mickey said, getting my name wrong immediately. I didn't care. I was about to ride down Main Street in Amsterdam with the centerfielder from Commerce, Oklahoma, the Commerce Comet, the clean-up hitter, the switch hitter, the American League's Most Valuable Player of 1962, Mickey Charles Mantle.

Mickey was real quiet at first as he put the car in neutral and as my Dad started up his car and began moving. The chain between the cars pulled tight and jolted us a little when Mickey's car started rolling. Mickey concentrated on steering his dead car as it followed after my dad down Route 5-S and through the left turn onto Route 30 North. Once we made the turn, though, Mickey relaxed and started asking me questions.

"Where are we, anyway?"

"This is Amsterdam," I said proudly. "The Rug City."

"The Rug City," he repeated with a laugh. "What the heck does that mean?"

"We make rugs here. A company called Mohasco. You never heard of it?"

"Never heard of it."

"We used to have a minor-league team here, too, called the Rugmakers. You must have heard of them. They were a Yankee farm team."

"When?"

"Back in the '40s, I think. Probably right before you came up to the majors."

"Never heard of 'em," he said. "No offense, of course."

"It's okay," I said. I didn't want him to feel bad. I couldn't believe he never heard of Amsterdam or the Rugmakers, though. Especially since he played for the Yankees.

While I was thinking about that, we crossed the bridge over the Mohawk River and turned right onto Main Street. The stores were all closed, but a lot of people were standing outside Brownie's Lunch, as usual. I was hoping to see somebody I knew, so I could wave and maybe they'd recognize Mickey Mantle driving the car. Didn't happen, though. Meanwhile, Mick was looking around, checking things out, and when we passed the Tryon Theater, he spoke again.

"*To Kill a Mockingbird* is playing here! What a great movie! Have you seen it yet?"

"No," I said, trying to be serious and have an adult conversation with him. "I don't like animal movies."

"It ain't about animals," he said. "It's about people. Yogi convinced a bunch of us to go see it when we were out in Detroit. You oughta go see it."

"Okay," I said, a little bit embarrassed, and then I told him about my favorite movie of all time. "Last summer, we saw your movie, *Safe at Home*, at that theater. "

"You saw that? How'd you like it?"

"I loved it. I saw it three times."

"Three times? Why'd you go three times?"

"I love watching you and Roger Maris hit home runs."

"Yeah, that was kinda fun," he said. By then, we were stopped at the red light at the bottom of Liberty Street.

"You go to school around here?" Mick asked.

"Yeah, I do. See that church up there on the left?" and I pointed down the street to Saint Mary's. "That's Saint Mary's, and I go to Saint Mary's Institute, which is right behind it. We're the Saint Mary's Gaels," I said proudly.

"Gaels?" he repeated and looked at me funny. We were riding by the front of the church then. "What's a Gael?"

"A Gael is . . . It's a . . . ." I didn't have the slightest idea what a Gael was. Nobody had ever asked me that before. And the nuns had never told us. Or, if they did, I guess I wasn't paying attention at the time. Finally, I just made up an answer.

"It's a special kind of angel," I said, hoping he wouldn't ask me any more about it.

"Oh, like the Los Angeles Angels?" he asked, laughing again.

"Yeah, that's it," I said, relieved.

"I hope you guys play better than they do. We hardly ever lose to them."

As we got close to Natale's Gas Station in the East End, Dad put his left signal light on. He pulled in and swung around between the front door of the station and the gas pumps. The place was dark and deserted. Dad got out of his car and said, "We'll unhook the chain and push your car over against that wall. I'll call Frank when we get home and let him know it's here."

After we got the chain off and the car in position, Mickey locked it up and gave Dad the keys.

"Don't you want to get your stuff out of the trunk?" Dad asked.

"The only thing I got in there is a spare tire."
"You don't have a suitcase or anything?"
"I wasn't planning on staying over. I figured I'd be back in New York by midnight at the latest."
"Okay. I'll leave your keys in the slot in the door, and we'll head out."

I got in the back seat this time, and Mick rode up front with Dad. As we were driving back down Main Street, Dad put the Yankee game on the radio. They were playing the Athletics in New York, and Ralph Terry was pitching. The Yanks led two to nothing in the sixth.

"When do you think you'll be able to play again, Mick?" Dad asked.

"The Major said I might be able to pinch hit this weekend. If it were up to me, I'd be playing tonight."

"How's your leg?" I asked him.

"It's as good as it's going to get. I'm ready."

"I was listening to the game the night you got hurt," I said. "I couldn't believe it."

"You couldn't believe it?" Mickey said. "I couldn't believe it myself. I was about to make the greatest catch of my career — and rob Brooks Robinson of a home run — when my spike gets hung up on that . . . that stupid wire fence in Baltimore."

It sounded like he really wanted to swear, but he didn't. Probably because I was there.

"You really think you would have caught it? Mel Allen said he didn't think you could have reached it."

"Mel Allen's a great announcer and a great guy," Mick said, "but he ain't never played center field."

"If you caught it, do you think it would have been a better catch than the one you made in Don Larsen's perfect game?"

"That was an easy one," he said. "All I had to do was run fast for that baby. This one, I had to run fast, jump, and climb a fence. And remember, they don't even have a warning track in Baltimore. If I hadn't a gotten hung up on that fence, I'd a caught it, too. Cheap home run for Brooksie."

"You hungry, Mick?" Dad asked as we got close to Brownie's Lunch again.

"I'm hungrier than a frog in heat," he answered.

What's a hot frog got to do with being hungry, I wondered, but I didn't ask. Ralph Terry retired the Athletics one, two, three on eight pitches.

Dad found a parking spot near the front of Brownie's, and we pulled in. This time, I noticed Uncle Harry in the crowd out front, and everybody was so busy handing him dollar bills that they didn't even pay attention to us. We walked in and took a booth near the window. Dad and Mick each slid in one side of the booth, and I had to make a fast decision. Not enough time to decide, though, so I quick knelt down to tie my sneakers and think.

Should I sit next to Dad, so I can look straight at Mickey while we eat? Or, should I sit next to Mickey, so it will look like we're best friends to anybody that comes in? While I was thinking this over and slowly tying my second sneaker, Mick was looking at the menu.

"What's good here?" he asked.

"Hot dog with the works — mustard, onions, and meat sauce. It's their specialty," Dad answered, "and we like to get a side order of fries with gravy."

"Sounds good to me," Mick said, as he put the menu down to look around.

Finally, I decided I wanted to sit right next to Mick. But, before I straightened up, Uncle Harry walked in the front door, bumped into me as he came to our booth, and slid in next to Mickey.

"How ya doin', guys?" Uncle Harry said without even looking at us. He was busy counting his money and checking his little notepad. I stood up and sat next to Dad, who said, "Mick, this is my brother Harry."

Uncle Harry was still working, though, so Dad had to nudge him. "Harry, say 'Hello' to Mick."

"Hello, Mick," he repeated, without looking up. "I'll be with you guys in a second."

Then, he finished counting his money and checking off all the numbers in his notepad.

While he was doing that, Brownie came over with three cups and a pitcher of coffee. He poured one for Uncle Harry without even asking and said, "Coffee for Harry." Then, he said, "Coffee for Pete," as he poured one for Dad.

"And coffee for Mick," Mickey filled in when he noticed Brownie's pause.

Brownie looked at Mick as if he knew him, but he looked puzzled, too, like he couldn't be sure, or like he was afraid to say something stupid. So, instead, he looked at me and said, "Let me guess. A big glass of chocolate milk for you?"

"Yes," I said politely but unbelievingly. I was dying to tell him and Uncle Harry to open their eyes and welcome Mickey Mantle to Amsterdam, but Dad was already giving our order. I kinda felt bad for Mickey because nobody was payin' that much attention to him. When Brownie left, though, Uncle Harry finished up, put his money in his billfold, and put his notepad in his shirt pocket.

"I'll get you later, Pete," he said to Dad, and then he put his hand out to shake with Mickey.

"What'd you say your name was?"

"Mick," Mickey answered, without giving his last name.

Uncle Harry looked down at Mickey's big hand, and, then, he looked Mickey straight in the eye and said, "I know you!"

Mickey got a goofy look on his face, like he'd been through this a million times.

"You're Mickey . . . Mickey . . . Mickey . . . — "

"Mantle," I wanted to say as Uncle Harry kept trying to come up with his last name. How could he not know? Finally, finally, finally, he finished.

"You're Mickey Rooney!" he said, proud as could be of himself for finally remembering.

I couldn't believe it. How could Uncle Harry be so stupid? Mickey was surprised at first, too, but, then, he cracked up. We all did.

"Mickey Rooney," Mick said in amazement. "Ain't nobody ever called me 'Mickey Rooney' before."

"That's because you ain't never been in Amsterdam, New York, before," Uncle Harry said, laughing like the little comedian he'd just named.

That's when I realized Uncle Harry wasn't as dumb as I thought, and he was just pulling Mickey's leg, just like he always teased me about being so tall and thin. "Big drink 'a water," he always called me.

Well, the next thing I knew, the food was on the table, and the three of them were swappin' stories like they were old war buddies. Later, while Uncle Harry was tellin' stories about the last time he got arrested, Dad slipped me a dime and told me to call Mom to tell her we'd be home soon, and that we'd be bringing a guest. Because I didn't want to miss anything, I sprinted to the phone booth back by the men's room and quickly dialed VI-2-6481 — Larry's number — by mistake.

"Tony's Funeral Parlor," his brother Charles said when he answered the phone.

"Charley, let me talk to Larry. It's Jumbo."

"He's busy watching *The Man from U.N.C.L.E.*"

"Tell him it's important."

I fished another dime out of my blue jeans while I waited, so I could call Mom next.

"Whattya want?" Larry said.

"You're not going to believe who's staying at our house tonight!"

"I thought you said this was important."

"Mickey Mantle."

"Yeah, okay. I gotta go."

"No, I'm serious. I'm down at Brownie's Lunch having hot dogs with him. His car broke down on 5-S, and we gave him a lift. His car's dead — "

And so was Larry's phone. He hung up on me; the creep. For a lousy rerun of *The Man from U.N.C.L.E.*

Then, when I called Mom, she didn't believe me either.

"Where are you guys?"

"We're down at Brownie's Lunch. We'll probably be done in about 10 or 15 minutes."

"Good, pick up some milk on the way home."

"All right, but I'm serious about bringing Mickey Mantle home."

"I'm serious about the milk, too." And she hung up.

When I got back to the table, Uncle Harry had his little pad out again and was explainin' the numbers game to Mickey.

"All you have to do is pick a number between one and a thousand. If it hits, you win $540 for every dollar you bet."

"Where's this number come from?"

"It's the last three numbers from the total handle for tonight's races at Saratoga Harness."

"How do I know you don't already know the number?"

"The races ain't over yet, Mick. Whatsa matter? You don't trust me?"

"This ain't the way we do it in Oklahoma."

"Forget Oklahoma. You ain't in Oklahoma. You're in Amsterdam."

"I know, the Rug City. Jimbo here filled me in on all that stuff."

While they were giving each other a hard time, Dad went up to the counter and paid Brownie for our food. I finished my french fries and chocolate milk.

"Seven. I want seven," Mickey said, finally, and he gave Uncle Harry a five-dollar bill. "And if I win, I want to see you before I leave tomorrow."

"Don't you worry about a thing," Uncle Harry said, as he went back to the phone booth to make a call of his own.

Then, when Mick realized Dad had already paid, he tried to give him a $20 bill on the way out the door.

"It's on me, Mick. You can treat next time we're in Oklahoma." Mick put the $20 bill in his pocket, but he winked at me and pointed, too, as if he were going to give me the money later.

"And don't give it to Jimbo, either," Dad said, laughing. Then, we piled into the car, stopped at Joe's Market for the milk, and headed home.

When we walked in the house, Mom, Kathy, and Marie were playing *Scrabble* in the dining room and eating popcorn. Anne, Jenny, and Peggy were already in bed. Dad walked in first and introduced Mick to everybody. Mom and the girls were all embarrassed because they had those ugly, pink curlers on their heads. Didn't seem to bother, Mick, though. He pulled up a chair next to Marie and tried to help her make a word. Mom and Dad excused themselves for a second and went upstairs to talk. I put the milk in the fridge and then sat down and ate some popcorn.

While Mick and Marie were looking over her letters, Kathy began peppering him with questions.

"Do you have any kids, Mr. Mantle?" she asked politely.

"I sure do," he said proudly. "I got four of the handsomest boys you've ever seen. How old are you?"

"I'm 13," she said, as if she were the only teenager in the world.

"You're too old for my boys," he said, as he pulled out his wallet and flashed their pictures. "Here's Mickey Junior! He just turned ten, and he's faster than a jackrabbit. Runs like the wind, that boy.

"This here is David. He's seven and a half, and he's sweet as can be, just like his Mom. Real polite all the time.

"This is Billy, named after my best friend, Billy Martin. Billy's four and a half, and he's kinda small for his age, but he's feisty, real feisty, just like his namesake.

"And here's Danny. He's the baby of the family. He's just turned three while we were down in Florida for spring training. He's a tough little guy, too. Always tryin' to keep up with his big brothers."

"Do you have any pictures of your wife?"

"Of course, I do. Here's Merlyn and me and the boys a few years ago after Danny was born. She's a beauty, isn't she? And a real sweetheart, too."

"Where are they now?"

Kathy was askin' a lot of questions, but Mick didn't seem to mind. Of course, Marie still wanted help with her *Scrabble* letters, so she was makin' faces.

"They're all down in Dallas, Texas. They used to stay in New Jersey with me during the summer months, but this year, we decided to let 'em all stay home. I don't get to see 'em as often, but it's a lot more fun for all of them to be with their friends at our swimming pool. I was down there for a couple weeks right after I hurt my leg."

Then, while Kathy was trying to think of another question, Mick said, "Hey, we can spell 'Dallas,'" and he took Marie's letters and put them on the board over a Double-Word score.

"No! You can't use proper nouns," Kathy announced immediately, just as Mom and Dad came back downstairs. Mom had removed her curlers.

"Okay, girls," Mom said to Marie and Kathy, "game's over; time for bed. You, too, Jim. Mr. Mantle's going to sleep in your bed, and you can sleep on the floor in the room with Anne, Jenny, and Peggy. I've already put a pillow and blanket in there for you."

"You don't have to kick him out of his bed on my account," Mick said. "I can sleep anywhere. Especially tonight. I'm whipped."

"No, you're a guest in our home, and you should have a bed and some privacy. He'll be fine. Besides, he'd be honored to know that you slept in his bed. Isn't that right, James Joseph *Michael*?"

I knew exactly where Mom was going with that one.

"Did he tell you, Mr. Mantle, that he chose Michael as his confirmation name two years ago because of you? He wanted to choose 'Mickey,' but we wouldn't let him. No offense, of course."

"Of course," Mickey said politely.

"Okay, you kids, get upstairs, and make sure you brush your teeth."

"Can we keep the game here until tomorrow?" Marie asked quietly, the first words she had spoken since we got home. She must have been winning.

"Yes, you may," Mom answered. "Now get going."

Kathy and Marie gave Mom and Dad a kiss good-night and went upstairs. Normally, I would have gone up with them without a fight, but I was trying to finagle a way to spend more time with Mick. So, when I saw Mom dumping the leftover popcorn in the garbage can, I pretended to be the boy who never forgets his chores.

"Here, Mom, let me do that for you. I have to put the garbage out tonight anyway."

On Sunday and Wednesday nights, I was always supposed to empty all the waste baskets and put the trash can out by the curb, so the garbage men could collect it in the morning. Usually, I'd forget until the morning, when I'd hear the truck outside my bedroom window, and I'd have to run out in my pajamas just to get the can to the curb on time. Tonight, for a change, I was Mr. Efficient.

Of course, Dad knew exactly what I was doing, and he smiled at me as he turned on the television to catch the news before going to bed. Kathy and Marie knew what I was doing, too, and they gave me grief about it when I emptied the waste basket in the upstairs bathroom.

"What a good little boy you are," Kathy said, "emptying all the waste baskets for your mother."

Marie, the quiet one downstairs, didn't waste any time either. "Here, Mommy, let Jimmy do that for you," she said sarcastically. "You are such a goody two-shoes, it's disgusting. How can you live with yourself?"

They couldn't get a rise out of me, though. I was still alive in the stay-up-as-late-as-you-can game. "Why don't you two go to sleep now like good little girls," I said sweetly and headed back downstairs.

When I got there, I heard Dad tell Mick that Frank Natale was going to check out the car and call by 8:00 in the morning. If it wasn't too serious, Mick could be on the road by nine. Praying for serious, I collected the rest of the downstairs garbage and went outside. As I carried the trash can down the driveway and walked back to the house, I heard Bernie's mom next door yell at him to take the garbage out before he went to bed. So I took my sweet time and waited for him.

"Hey, Bernie," I said when he finally came out. "Guess who's staying at our house tonight?"

"Your grandma's staying over again. Big deal."

"No, really, this is a big deal. Guess again."

"Just tell me; I ain't got all night."

Bernie wasn't really a tough guy, but he liked to pretend that he was, and I played along with him.

"Mickey Mantle."

"Yeah, okay," and he started carrying his trash can down the driveway.

"I'm serious."

"I got five dollars right here that says he ain't stayin' at your house."

Bernie had a morning paper route delivering the Schenectady *Gazette*, so he thought he was hot stuff because he pulled in $15 a week. He even dropped his trash can and pulled out a brand new five-dollar bill just to show off.

"You're on," I said in my best Uncle Harry gambling voice.

"You ain't got five bucks to bet."

He was right, of course, so I had to think fast.

"I'll put up my um . . . um . . . my um . . . —"

"How 'bout that new Stan Musial bat your dad gave you for your birthday?"

"All right," I said confidently, even though the bat was worth ten bucks at least. That was a mistake. Bernie backed off when he saw how eager I was to make the bet.

"Where is he right now?" he asked.

"We got a bet or not?"

"I ain't bettin' ya. I just want to see him. What's he doin' at your house, anyway?" He started walking toward the downstairs window.

"His car broke down, and we gave him a ride."

Bernie couldn't quite see into the living room, so he dragged his trash can over to the window and stood on top. I held the can, so he wouldn't fall over, and then I heard him say in a loud whisper, "Holy crap! That's unbelievable. Can I come in and see him?"

"Not now. It's too late."

"How long's he gonna be here?"

"He's stayin' overnight, and he'll probably leave as soon as his car's fixed tomorrow."

Bernie hadn't taken his eyes off him. "Does anybody else know he's here?"

"I told Larry on the phone, but he didn't believe me."

"Good. Don't tell anybody else."

"Why not?"

"Bernie! What are you doing out there?" His mother's yelling almost made him fall off the garbage can, but I held him up.

"I'll be right in, Ma," he yelled back after he jumped down. "I'm helping Jumbo with his garbage."

Then, he spoke to me again. "Let's keep him to ourselves. I won't tell anybody if you don't."

"Okay, it's a deal."

"Good, I'll be over first thing in the morning."

"Bernie!"

"I'm comin', Ma. I'm comin'."

He put his garbage can on the curb, and we both went inside. They were just finishin' up the weather on TV, so I sat down to wait for the sports. Mom gave me a look that said, "What are you still doing up?" but she and I both knew Dad would say it was okay.

"Do you think they won?" I asked Mick.

"Probably. The A's aren't that great, and Ralph's been talkin' to the ball pretty good again this year."

"He talks to the ball?"

"Oh, yeah. All the time. Before the game. During the game. After the game. It works for him, too — most of the time. We really got on his case in '61 after he gave up that home run to Mazerowski on the last pitch of the 1960 Series. But he's been gettin' even with us this year, telling us all about the last pitch in last year's Series when Willie McCovey lined out to Bobby Richardson."

When he said all that, I flashed back immediately to where I was when those things happened. When Mazerowski's home run beat the Yankees in the 1960 World Series, we were shootin' hoops in Larry's back yard with the radio on in the garage. We were all so sure that the Yankees would pull it out after they tied the Pirates in the top of the ninth. Then, when Mazerowski ended it, Larry kicked his basketball over the garage and down onto Academy Street. Our game ended just like that. Everybody went home. I cried when I got to my bedroom. I bet everybody else did too.

Then, last year, I was helpin' Rick Fetterly deliver his papers when Ralph Terry was on the mound again in the last game of the Series against the Giants. We stopped at Steve Gorman's house, and he let us in to watch the last inning with him. The Giants were down by one, Willie Mays was on second, and McCovey was at the plate. I wanted them to walk McCovey because I thought he'd beat us for sure. And he almost did. He scared the daylights out of all of us when he hit that screaming meemie toward right field. But good old Bobby Richardson, the Yankee second baseman, stepped in front of it like there was nothin' to it, and the game was over.

Now the Yankees were tryin' to win their fourth straight pennant and their third straight World Series, and they were about seven games ahead of the White Sox with less than 30 games to go. Everything looked great, and Mick would be back in the lineup soon, too. All right!

After the commercials, we found out that the Yankees did win, but it was closer than we expected. Ralph Terry got the win, but he needed a home run by Tom Tresh in the bottom of the ninth to pull it out. Then, it was bedtime.

"Time to hit the hay," Dad said, as he turned off the TV.

I tried one more delaying tactic.

"Can't we just watch Johnny Carson's monologue?"

"No. You go to bed and get a good night's sleep. You got a ball game tomorrow night, don't ya?"

"Yeah."

"Tell him, Mick, how important it is to get enough sleep the night before a game."

"Your dad's right, Jimbo," he said with a yawn. "I'm about ready to hit the hay myself. It's been a long day."

"What were you doing up here today anyway?" I asked.

Mickey had a big smile on his face. He looked at Dad and smiled and said, "This boy doesn't want to go to bed, does he?" They both laughed. Then Mickey answered — sort of.

"Tell ya what I'll do. Tomorrow, I'll let you guess why I was up here, and I'll tell ya if you're right. But for now, you have to listen to your dad."

"All right," I said, my mind spinning with possibilities. "You came up here to scout me for the Yankees, didn't you?" I said, laughing, as I walked up the stairs.

They laughed again, and Mom told me to be quiet and not to wake up the girls. I brushed my teeth, and when I came out of the bathroom, Mom, Dad, and Mick were still talking downstairs. I listened for a few minutes hoping to hear why Mick was in Amsterdam, but they were talking about the car again, so I went to bed trying to figure out this mystery.

Maybe he had to speak at a banquet or something like that while he's on the disabled list. Or maybe he was scouting someone for the Yankees. Or maybe he just felt like taking a ride. Dad does that all the time with us.

AMSTERDAM
HIGH
SCHOOL

Chapter Two

The next thing I knew, it was Thursday morning, and Anne, Jenny, and Peggy were all awake and wondering why I was sleeping in their room. Peggy was standing up in her crib, just looking at me, but Anne, who was still in her bed said, "What are you doing in here?" and Jenny came back into the bedroom and asked, "Who's that sleeping in your bed?"

"Mickey Mantle," I mumbled, hardly believing it myself.

"Yeah, sure," said Anne, and she threw a pillow at me.

"It's Uncle Harry, isn't it?" said Jenny, who usually believed anything I told her. "What's he doing here?"

"It's not Uncle Harry; it's Mickey Mantle. He came last night to see if I want to play for the Yankees when I graduate from high school."

They all laughed, but the story sounded so good, I kept going.

"He said the Yankees have searched all over the country for someone as good as I am and who will be ready to step in when he retires. He said they'll pay me $100,000 now if I sign a contract and another $100,000 when I play my first year in the majors. So, if you girls are good to me, I might even buy you those new bikes you were looking at over at City Cycle last week."

"Will you buy me the pink one with the horn and the big basket on the front?" Jenny asked seriously.

"Whatever you want," I promised, "but you'll have to do the dishes for me when it's my turn."

"It's a deal," she agreed.

Then, I got up and went to the bathroom. When I came out, I tiptoed down the hall to peek into my room. I didn't want to wake Mick up. When I looked in, though, the bed was empty. I couldn't believe it. He couldn't have gotten up so fast. Jenny had just seen him in there. I even looked in the closet. Nothing. Just as I turned back to the hall, he popped out from behind the bedroom door and wrestled me to the bed. He was so strong, I couldn't move.

"A hundred-thousand dollars a year," he said laughing. "That's as much as I make, and you're not even going to play for another six or seven years. You must not really be awake yet, Jimbo. You're still dreaming."

"Where were you?" I asked, trying to change the subject and cover up my embarrassment. I couldn't believe he heard the whole thing.

"I was spyin' on you. The Yankees sent me up here to see if you were really good enough to take my place. Some of the things they told me to check on were whether you got up early, strike one; whether you always told the truth, strike two; and whether you were strong enough to play in the big leagues. C'mon, let's see you get out of this one. You got two strikes on you."

I tried to get up, but I couldn't move. And he wasn't working hard at all to keep me down.

"Strike three, you're out!" he laughed again. Finally, he let me up and said, "C'mon, Jimbo, let's go eat breakfast."

He walked out first, and I followed him down the stairs. He had bare feet, his hair was messed up, and his shirt was hangin' out over his pants, but he still looked great. Maybe if I did more pushups, I thought, I could have arms and shoulders like his. No wonder he hit the ball so far.

When we got downstairs, Dad had everything out in the dining room waiting for us: eggs, sausage, toast, juice, coffee, doughnuts, and the Schenectady *Gazette*. I couldn't believe it. Usually on Saturdays, Dad will get up and cook breakfast for us like this, but even then, we never ate breakfast in the dining room; we always ate breakfast at the counter in the kitchen. Then, I noticed it was only 7:30. I was up even earlier than usual. I was about to tell Mick about this, but he was already eating a sausage, and Dad was showing him the box score from last night's game and getting ready to go to work.

"Okay, Mick. I think you're all set. I'll call later when I find out what's wrong with your car. If you need anything, you know who to talk to," and he looked at me.

"Don't worry, Dad," I said confidently, as he went out the back door. "I'll take good care of him."

"What do you have going on today, Jimbo?" Mick asked.

"We usually play ball over at the Cage in the morning and then at Academy Street School in the afternoon."

"Didn't your dad say you have a game tonight, too?"

Before I had a chance to answer, Mom jumped in. She knew exactly what I was thinking. "Jim, Mr. Mantle will probably have to return to New York today. He won't be able to come to your game."

"But what if his car's not ready?"

"Frank will probably have that car ready to go before lunchtime today."

"I sure hope so," said Mick. "Not that I don't want to see your game, Jimbo, but I really do need to get back to New York as soon as possible. Otherwise, they'll forget who I am."

"Yeah, fat chance," I said, trying not to sound too disappointed. "Will you at least come over to the Cage this morning and play with us?" I asked in desperation.

"Once your dad calls with news about the car, I might be able to do that before I go. But only on one condition."

"What's that?"

"You have to promise me that you and your dad will come down and watch a game in Yankee Stadium. I'll leave free tickets for you at the main gate."

"It's a deah," I said, talking with my mouth full and with my Mom scolding me.

"I think he said, 'It's a deal,' Mr. Mantle," she translated, "though he knows better than to talk with his mouth full. They'd love to come to a game in New York. They've been talking about it all summer, but they just haven't gotten around to it. In the meantime, I'd like young James Joseph Michael here to finish eating and bring that garbage can in off the curb before he goes anywhere."

"You heard your ma, Jimbo. Get movin'."

"Yes, sir!" I said, and I ate as quick as I could, while Mickey tried to make small talk with Anne, Jenny, and Peggy, who were all asleep when he arrived. Anne and Jenny, though, were acting shy and quiet, so Mick played quite a bit with Peggy, who was sitting in her high chair.

As soon as I finished eating, I brought my dishes to the kitchen, and I overheard Marie crying.

"What's a matter with you?" I asked.

I wanted Mr. Mantle to finish playing *Scrabble* with us, and you went and asked him to play baseball with you. You wrecked everything."

"He doesn't want to play *Scrabble*. He's a baseball player, for cryin' out loud, not a *Scrabble* player."

"Mom," Marie said, when Mom walked in the kitchen, "Didn't you say we could finish that *Scrabble* game today?"

"Yes, honey. We can finish right after we clean up."

"But James Joseph Michael went and asked Mr. Mantle to play baseball, and Mr. Mantle said, 'Yes.'"

"Well, maybe he can play a few turns with us before he goes."

"Yeah, sure."

I washed my plate and glass in the sink, left them in the drainboard, and ran out the back door to bring in the empty garbage can. As I did, I could hear Marie yelling again in the kitchen.

"Mom, he didn't dry his dishes or put them away like he's supposed to."

When I got to the front of the house, I saw Larry walking up the street, like he usually did, to get us all ready for our morning ball game. Usually, he'd get me and Bernie, and together we'd go up our side of the street and get the Dufresne boys first, then Paul Towers, Angelo Verderesee, Dave Hammond, and Mark Dunn. At the top of Wilson, we'd cross over and go back down the other side and pick up the Geibs, Mike Booth, Matt Kenyon, and the three Fetterly brothers. Sometimes, we'd get a few guys from Bunn Street and Glen Avenue, too, on our way to the Cage. Most days, we had 15 to 20 guys, and we'd all walk or ride our bikes over.

Rick Geib and Hugh Fetterly were the oldest, so, if they came, they got to pick the teams. I never got to pick because I wasn't that old or that good yet, but I was usually one of the first five or six guys chosen. And even though I played first base for Slezaks, I never played first base in the Cage. I always played the outfield, usually center field in honor of number seven. I'd gladly play left or right today, though, if he really showed up like he said he would. I figured he probably would, too, because those girls would drive him nuts at the house, especially once he found out he had to play *Scrabble* all morning. My only worry was that his car would be ready soon and that he'd go back to New York City before he had a chance to play with us.

"Well, where is he?" Larry asked when he got close.

"He's probably upstairs in the bathroom."

"Yeah, sure. And I suppose he's going to play ball with us this morning, too?"

"He said he'd come over later, after he finds out about his car."

"Yeah, okay. Where's Bernie? Did he come out yet?"

"No."

Then, just as we were walking up the driveway to put the garbage can on the back porch where it belonged, Bernie came out of his house and asked excitedly, "Where is he? What's going on?"

Before I had a chance to answer, Larry laughed at him sarcastically.

"You believe him? You really think Mickey Mantle is here in Amsterdam?"

"I saw him with my own eyes."

"Then, you need these," Larry said, as he took off his glasses and pretended to offer them to Bernie. "C'mon, let's go see who wants to play today."

"Listen," I said, holding Larry back for a second. "I got a great idea. Let's play our side of Wilson Avenue plus Bunn Street against the other side of Wilson Avenue and Glen Avenue. That way, if Mick does show up later, he'll definitely be on our side when he gets there. It'll be great."

"That's a great idea," Bernie agreed. "Is he really coming to play with us?"

"He said he'd stop over once he finds out about his car."

"That's great. Okay, let's not tell anybody else he's here. Let's just say you had a family friend stay at your house last night, and when he shows up, he's on our side. They'll go crazy when they see who it is."

"You guys have already gone crazy," Larry said disgustedly. "C'mon, let's go."

Larry started off to get some of the others, while Bernie and I dragged behind.

"How come he doesn't believe you?" Bernie asked.

"Same reason you didn't believe me last night."

"How'd you talk Mick into playing with us?"

"He asked what was going on, and I told him. Then, I just asked him if he'd come over and play for a while."

"All right. C'mon, let's catch up to Larry to make sure we get this game set up the way we want it."

Larry had already gotten Pat and Paul to play and was knocking on Angelo's front door. When Angelo found out what Bernie and I wanted the sides to be, he flipped out and started screaming at Larry.

"What are you guys, nuts? We can't beat them if we give them the Geibs and all the Fetterly brothers. They'll kill us."

"Talk to the organizers. It was their idea."

I was ready to tell Angelo our secret just to shut him up, but Bernie cut me off.

"Will you stop being such a baby? Just cuz they're a little older than we are don't mean nothin'. Besides, we'll be playin' against them next year in Rookie League. You might as well get used to it."

"Yeah, well, I ain't pitchin'; I'll tell ya that right now. Hughie Fetterly practically took my head off with a line drive last time I pitched to him."

"Don't you worry about Hughie Fetterly," Bernie said. "He won't be able to touch my new curve ball."

"Yeah, cuz you can't get it over the plate."

While they argued, we rounded up the rest of the guys, and nobody else complained. The Geibs and the Fetterlys both thought it was a great idea to play one side of the street against the other. Of course, they thought they'd be batting all morning, but they didn't know about our secret weapon.

When we got to the bottom of the street and were finally ready to head over to the Cage, I ran back to the house to check on Mick. He hadn't showered yet and was playing *Scrabble* with the girls. I couldn't believe it. I wanted to scream at him and the girls, but I didn't want any more strikes against me, so I put on my altar-boy face and spoke very politely.

"Excuse me. I just wanted you to know that we're heading over to the Cage now. I'll leave my bike in the driveway for you with my dad's glove on the handlebars. All you have to do is go to the bottom of the street, turn right on Bunn Street, and go straight across until you see us in the Cage up by the high school."

"Okay, Jimbo. Once I get the call, I'll be over."

"I already made sure you'll be on my team."

"Shortstop?"

"You serious?"

"Why not?"

"Well . . . um . . . uh — "

"You think just because they made me an outfielder that I can't play shortstop?"

"I heard you made a lot of throwing errors."

"I was young and wild then. Not so anymore. You put me at shortstop, and I'll do better than Tony Kubek. Guaranteed."

"All right. If you say so."

"See ya over there," and he went back to his *Scrabble* game.

I had to run halfway to the Cage to catch up with everybody, and once I saw who else had shown up, I knew we were in for a tough game. All the Fetterly brothers showed up and so did Joe Merendo. It looked like the big kids against the little kids. The only older guys we had on our team were Tim Welch and Paul Towers, and neither one of them was that good. Plus, the other team had one more guy than we did.

"We'll give ya Bobby, if ya want," Hugh Fetterly said of his youngest brother.

"Nah," I said. "We'll be okay. A friend of our family is coming over later, and we'll take him when he comes."

"All right, we'll let you guys bat first, then. Otherwise, you might not get to hit," he laughed, and so did all the others on his team.

Even Bernie looked a little nervous, and Angelo came up to me and said, "Is your friend any good?"

"He's as good as Mickey Mantle," I bragged, knowing no one would believe me. Except Bernie, of course.

We managed to score two runs in the first inning, but they got four. In the second, we got three; they got five. They were killing us. It seemed like we were out in the field forever. And boy was it hot. Tim Welch said he heard the temperature was supposed to reach 100 by lunch time.

I kept looking down the road from my position in center field to see if Mick was coming. It was about 11:30, and we were behind 18-11 when I finally saw my bike moving towards us. By then, the Fetterly boys were ready to call it a day. They were the only family I knew that had air conditioning, and they couldn't wait to get home to it. When Hugh made the last out for his team, he called, "Three outs and that's it. I'm going home."

"What if we tie it or go ahead?" I asked, as I ran by him to prepare to hit.

"You guys don't have a prayer."

"But what if we do? Will you stick around for your half of the inning or not?"

"It's too hot, Jumbo."

"So you don't want your last at bats?"

"Tell ya what; if you guys tie the score or go ahead — which will never happen — you win. You guys get your last at bats, and that's it."

"Red, white, and blue, no changee?" I asked, to make sure he was serious.

"Red, white, and blue, no changee," he agreed.

I couldn't believe it. Just about everything was falling perfectly into place. "Wait, there's one more thing," I said.

"Whaaattt?"

I pointed to Mick who was still too far away to be recognizable and said, "You gotta let him hit this inning, even though he hasn't played in the field yet." That was one of our standard rules. Anybody who came late couldn't bat unless he played at least one full inning in the field.

"All right, all right. C'mon, let's get going. I'm dying out here."

Paul Towers was up first for us, and he popped out to Joey Merendo at shortstop. Dave Hammond and Pat Dufresne were our seventh and eighth hitters, and if they made outs, the game would be over even before we got to the ninth position in the order, which is where Mick had to hit.

"Is that your cousin from Herkimer?" Larry asked, when he saw Mick getting closer on my bike.

"No, it ain't my cousin from Herkimer. I told you who was comin'."

Larry still didn't believe me, and I couldn't blame him. Mick had put on a pair of my dad's green work pants, an old pair of sneakers, and a softball shirt from the Dew Drop Inn. He kinda looked like my cousin from Herkimer. Larry forgot all about the guy on the bike and tried to talk Dave into getting a hit.

"C'mon, Dave. Pretend that baseball is Joe Merendo's head and crush it."

Fortunately, Dave hit a ground ball just past Mike Booth at second base. Then, Bobby Fetterly misjudged Pat's pop-fly to right, so we had two guys on and only one out, when Mickey rolled to a stop on my bike just outside the Cage.

"You gotta get a new bike, Jimbo. They come with gears now, ya know, so it's easier to peddle."

Bernie and I were grinning like idiots, and Angelo Verderesee almost had a cat. "It is Mickey Mantle. Holy Toledo!"

While Mickey was leaning my bike against the fence with the other bikes, Angelo ran out and practically tackled him.

"Easy, big fella," Mick said to Angelo, the smallest guy in the group. Then, he picked Angelo up like he was a bag of bats, and he threw him over his shoulder. Angelo was laughing like crazy, and the game had stopped. Most of the older guys were just staring. They couldn't believe it. But when Hughie Fetterly ran all the way in from center field to shake the Mick's hand, everybody else did, too.

And Mick was great. He put Angelo down, shook everybody's hand, and had a greeting for everybody, too.

"Hey, Pardner. Hey, Champ. Hey, Big Guy, Lefty, Red."

He even gave Bobby Fetterly a hard time for misjudging Pat Dufresne's fly ball to right. "You gotta know where the ball's going before you start to chase it," he said.

Bobby usually got mad when his older brothers tried to tell him something like that, but he didn't give the Mick a hard time. "Yes, sir," he said, like a little toy soldier.

Then, when everybody was unsure what should happen next, Mick jumped right in. "Well, what's going on here? Are we playing a game or not?"

"You're up," I said. "We got two guys on, one out, and we're down by seven."

"But I haven't played the field yet," he said.

"It's all right, Mick," Rick Geib said, as he ran back on the field. He couldn't wait to pitch to him.

"Here, use my bat," said Mike Booth, as he handed him the new black bat he had just bought the day before at Sievert's Sporting Goods. We were all pretty surprised because Mike wouldn't even let any of us use the bat yet.

But Mick looked at the bat, laughed, and handed it back to Mike. "You want me to use a Rocky Colavito model? I'm sorry, son, but don't you guys have any of my bats around here?"

"I got one," Omeo said, and he handed his Mickey Mantle model to the Mick himself. Nobody but Omeo used that bat any more, because it had already been cracked twice. Each time, Omeo brought it home, put screws in it, and taped it up, so it really wasn't that bad. Mick didn't mind.

"I think this baby's got a few hits left in it. C'mon. Play ball."

Dave and Pat went back to second and first, and everybody else took their positions in the field. Since Rick Geib was a righty, Mick stepped in to bat lefty.

The right-field fence looked awful close when he stepped up to the plate. The Cage was a rectangular field fenced in between the high-school football field, the tennis courts, and the road. Some days, we played with home plate near the road, so the left-field fence was close, and most of us could try to hit home runs into the football field. Every once in a while, though, we played with home plate near the football field, so the left-handed batters could try to hit homers over the fence to the road. It was one of those days.

When Bobby Fetterly got back to right field, he had his back against the fence, and his brother Hughie was practically against the fence in center field, too.

"Why don't you guys climb the fence and sit on top?" Joe Merendo yelled out to them.

"Won't do any good," Bernie yelled back. "This is home run number 416 coming up."

Mick stepped out of the box, looked back at Bernie and asked: "How'd you know that?"

"Easy. It's on your baseball card." He pulled Mick's 1963 card out of his back pocket and showed it to him. "You had 404 at the end of last year, and you've only got 11 this year."

"Only 11!" Mick yelled, as he dropped the bat and put Bernie in a headlock. "I've been on the disabled list for almost two months, ya know."

"I know. I know," Bernie said, laughing. "I'm sorry."

"Kids!" Mickey said, laughing himself, and he grabbed his bat again and stepped back up to the plate.

Meanwhile, Rick Geib was getting himself all pumped up to face the Mick. He stared at Matt Kenyon behind the plate as if he were looking for a sign, but everybody knew he was going to try and throw it as fast as he could. Sure enough, he threw a high, hard one that was probably out of the strike zone, but Mick swung anyway and didn't quite catch all of it. At first, it looked like a high pop-fly that might not get over the fence, but the ball just kept going and going. Nobody said a word, as we watched and waited. The ball cleared the fence easily and landed a second later on the other side of the road, up near the backstop on one of the softball fields.

We all started cheering, and Mickey started jogging around the bases. Bernie was yelling "416, 416, 416." Bobby Fetterly squeezed himself through the hole in the fence in right field and ran across the road and up the small hill to get the ball. We all ran up to home plate and shook Mickey's hand when he crossed. I know I felt like a major leaguer just being there.

Of course, we were still down by four runs, 18 to 14, but we had the top of the order coming up. Angelo, who was one of the few left-handed hitters in our gang, was up, and he was trying like crazy to impress Mickey. Angelo knew he couldn't reach the fence, but he tried anyway. He fouled off two pitches in the strike zone and then swung wildly and missed at a pitch that was way over his head. Two outs. We were down to our last batter.

Bernie took a big cut at the first pitch and hit a screamer to the gap in left center for a double. I was up next. I knew I could never reach the left-field fence, so I just tried to meet the ball, and I hit a grounder up the middle for a single. Bernie scored to make it 18-15.

Larry didn't care how far the left-field fence was. He wanted to hit a home run in front of the Mick in the worst way. He missed twice by a long shot, and everybody was beggin' him to just try and get a single, so the game wouldn't be over, but he wouldn't listen. Luckily, on his third swing, he nicked the ball and hit a slow squibbler toward Omeo at third. He tried to barehand it and throw like Clete Boyer, but there was no way Omeo was going to throw out Larry. He flew down the first-base line and beat the throw by a mile.

We had runners on first and second and two outs, and Tim Welch was up. He hit an easy ground ball to Joe Merendo at short. Joe was usually a pretty good fielder. This time, though, I think he was trying to show off. When he fielded the ball, he had an easy force out at second, but, instead, he gunned the ball as hard as he could over to Pete Geib at first. His throw was about three feet over Pete's head, and the ball rattled noisily against the chain-link fence. I might have been able to score on the play, but I didn't want to take a chance, so we had the bases loaded for Paul Towers, who had already made the first out in the inning.

While all this was going on, Mick was walking up and down the first-base line encouraging us and teasing us at the same time.

"Jimbo, you should have scored on that play. I'll get your bike out to you next time."

"Hey, Lefty," he said to Pete Geib, after Joe's throw went over Pete's head at first base. "You gotta get up in the air and get those."

When Paul Towers got to the plate to hit, everybody could tell he was real nervous, especially with the bases loaded and all.

"Don't make another out," Larry yelled.

"Another out?" Mickey yelled back and rushed up to home plate to call time out. "You mean to tell me," he said to Paul, "you already made an out in this inning?"

Paul shook his head yes, but he was laughing, too, because Mick was jabbing him in the stomach.

"Do you know what happens on the Yankees if you make two outs in one inning?"

Paul shook his head the other way this time.

"You gotta buy drinks for everybody after the game. Do you have any money?"

Paul shook his head no again.

"Well, then, you better get a hit, big boy."

Mickey's teasing must have helped because Paul drilled a single to left, and two runs scored. That made it 18-17. Now, I was afraid, we'd go ahead and win before Mick had another chance to hit. Fortunately, Mike Booth bobbled Dave Hammond's ground ball to second, and Pat Dufresne knocked in the tying run with a line drive to shortstop. Joey Merendo was just barely able to get his glove on the ball, but he couldn't hold on to it or throw anybody out on the play, either. That gave us a tie game with the bases loaded, and Mickey Mantle coming up to bat. I got goose bumps watching him go up to the plate again, and I bet everybody else did, too.

This time, though, Hughie Fetterly called "time out" and came running in from center field. "Rick," he yelled, "we can't let you pitch to him again. We gotta make him bat right-handed this time."

"But, I'll get him out. I promise."

"I don't think so. Switch places with your brother. At least we'll have a chance. That right-field fence is too short for him."

When Mickey saw that they were bringing in Pete Geib from first to pitch to him, he moved over from the left-hander's batting box to switch hit and bat right-handed."

"It ain't gonna matter, ya know," he said, flexing his muscles and pointing to the left-field fence with his bat. "I can reach that fence. Matter of fact, you better tell those tennis players to stay awake out there. You need any warmups, Lefty?"

"Just a couple."

I knew exactly what Pete was thinking out there. Not only did he want to strike out the great Mickey Mantle, but he also wanted to show up his older brother who had given up Mick's home run to right.

"All right, I'm ready," he said, after throwing three hard fastballs to get warmed up.

But Mick was ready, too. He had watched Pete throw and was taking practice swings with each pitch. I couldn't wait to see what was going to happen, and I didn't have to wait long.

Pete took a full windup and fired a fastball right down the pipe. Mick locked in on it and launched it to deep left field just like he promised. This one, though, was not a high pop-fly. This was a rocket that screamed off his bat and startled the tennis players who had to be 400 feet away. They didn't have to worry. The ball cleared both the fence separating our field from the tennis courts and the fence separating the tennis courts from the road. The ball bounced in the middle of the road and skipped into the parking lot at the new McNulty School.

"Way to go, Pedro," Rick Geib yelled at his younger brother. "I coulda done that."

We were going crazy again, as Mick rounded the bases. Dave Hammond was so excited, he did cart wheels all the way to home plate from third base. This time, everybody from both teams came in and gathered around Mick again. As he crossed the plate after his slow trot around the bases, the 12:00 noon siren from the high school sounded, meaning most of us had to head home for lunch. The game was over, and we won 22-18.

On the way home from the Cage, everybody was asking Mick all kinds of questions.

"Who's the best pitcher you ever faced?"

"Would you rather hit right-handed or left-handed?"

"What's the longest home run you ever hit?"

Instead of riding my bike, Mick let me take it, and he walked with us down Bunn Street. And everybody who had bikes with them walked their bikes back home, so they could be closer to Mick. He answered all the questions, too, but, whenever he answered a question, he asked the same one back. So, after he said Sandy Koufax was the best he'd ever seen, though he'd only faced him in spring training, he asked Bernie about the toughest pitcher he'd ever faced.

"Mike Kachan," Bernie answered. Mike was a lefty on Columbians who threw real hard, just like Koufax.

Then, after Mick told us he'd rather hit righty than lefty, he asked if any of us were switch-hitters. Larry said he was, but we all started laughing because we knew he was lying.

"Yeah, he's a switch-hitter," Joe Merendo said. "He can strike out either way — right-handed or left-handed."

Then, Mick said the longest home run he ever hit was the one he hit in May that almost went right out of Yankee Stadium. He said if it hadn't hit the facade, they estimated that it would have gone over 600 feet. Unfortunately, he looked right at me then and said, "What's the longest home run you ever hit, Jimbo?"

Everybody laughed again. "He ain't got one yet," Larry said. "Not in a real game, anyway."

I tried to tell Mick about how I almost hit the roof of the factory behind the Academy Street playground, but everybody said that didn't count because it wasn't a real game; it wasn't a Little League game.

Amazingly, though, Mick stuck up for me and said I'd probably get my first one "tonight."

"Are you going to be there, Mick?" Matt Kenyon asked because he knew I was playing against his team.

"No. I gotta head back soon," Mick answered, "but I might just tell old Jimbo here how to hit those tape-measure home runs before I leave."

"Tell me, too," Angelo pleaded, as we turned the corner to go up Wilson Avenue. By then, a lot of the guys had said good-by to Mick and shook his hand one more time.

"Sorry, Squirt," Mick laughed. "I can only tell this secret to the guy who's going to replace me in center field when I retire."

I got scared for a second, then, because I thought Mick might tell everybody about my bragging that morning, but he didn't. He just kinda looked at me and smiled as we walked up the driveway for lunch.

Chapter Three

When Mick and I walked in the house, Mom had lunch all ready for us. She had made a grilled cheese sandwich for each of us, with a slice of pickle on the side and a big pile of potato chips — my favorite meal. We sat down immediately with the girls to begin eating, but Mom wouldn't let us get away with anything.

"Did you wash your hands, young man?" she said to me, and Mickey responded as if she were talking to him.

"Can you believe we forgot to wash our hands?" he said, as he got up and lifted me out of my chair and pushed me towards the downstairs bathroom. I could tell he was really starting to feel comfortable in our house, and I think he was feeling good about his home runs, too. Instead of seriously washing his hands in the bathroom, he kept pretending to splash me accidentally. He'd get his hands wet, shake them off in my face, and say, "Oh, I'm sorry, Jimbo. I didn't mean to get you wet." Then, he'd laugh and do it again. I couldn't believe it.

During lunch, we heard that Mom won the *Scrabble* game after all and that the girls were going to walk down to school after lunch to see who their teachers were for the upcoming school year. The nuns always posted the class lists on the front doors of the school on August 1 to get everyone thinking about school way ahead of time. I didn't mind finding out who my teacher would be for the year, but I wasn't about to walk to school while Mick was still around. I'd wait until after he left for good.

"What was your favorite subject in school, Mr. Mantle?" Marie asked shyly.

"That's a good question," he said without answering. "What's yours, Kathy?"

"I like English," Marie said, ignoring the fact that Mick got her name wrong. Kathy wouldn't let his mistake go by, though.

She chirped in with, "I'm Kathy, and she's Marie."

"And what's your favorite subject, Kathy?" he asked her, probably knowing that they all wanted to talk at once.

"I like math, but I'm not very good at it."

"Yeah, she likes it," said Marie, "because Peter Thomas sat behind her last year and whispered to her all the time."

"He did not," she protested.

DEW DROP
INN

"Did too. Nancy Dufresne told me all about it."

While Mick and I polished off our sandwiches, the girls rambled on and on about who liked who, who they wanted as their teachers, and who they wanted in their classes with them. Mom made more sandwiches for Mick and me, and then the phone rang. It was Dad, and he asked to speak to Mick.

Sometimes, Dad came home and had lunch with us, but he must have been down at Natale's Garage checking on Mick's car. I assumed the end was near, and Mick would be on his way back to New York after lunch. Not before he tells me how to hit home runs, though, I thought, as I waited for him to speak.

"Oh, you're kiddin'?" he said. "How long will that take?"

I couldn't believe my good luck. His car still wasn't ready, and he'd have to hang around even longer. "All right," I whispered and stuffed a handful of potato chips in my mouth, so I wouldn't give myself away.

"Why so long?" he asked. Even the girls were silent and listening now.

"Yeah. I guess it'll be okay as long as I make it back to New York some time tonight."

We got him for this afternoon, too, I thought happily and maybe even for tonight's game.

"Jimbo's been great. Your whole family has been super. All right, I'll talk to you later," and he hung up.

As he explained everything to Mom, I found out that not only was his fuel pump bad, but his timing belt had to be replaced, too. I didn't know what any of that meant, of course, except that by the time they got all the parts they needed from a place in Albany and put everything in, they figured the car wouldn't be done till about five or six o'clock.

"That's too bad," Mom said. "Do you need to call anyone in your family or in New York?"

"I probably should," he answered, and he started going through his wallet, looking for the right phone numbers. While he made his calls, Bernie showed up on the back porch, and I quietly told him the good news.

"So what's he gonna do all afternoon?" he asked.

"I don't know. Why don't we ask him if he wants to play against the wall with us at Academy?"

"You think he would?"

"It's better than sittin' here all afternoon doin' nothin'."

"All right, you ask him."

"If I do and he says 'Yes,' he's on my team."

"You're really hoggin' him all to yourself, aren't you?"

"Tell you what. Next time he comes to Amsterdam, he can stay at your house and be on your team every time."

"Yeah, like he'll ever be here again, you big jerk."

When we walked in, Mick was still on the phone, and he must have been talkin' to one of his kids, because he was tellin' him all about the home runs he hit this morning. Bernie and I walked into the living room and sat down and watched a Shirley Temple movie with the girls.

"Isn't Mom making you go to the playground this afternoon?" I asked them.

"It's too hot," Kathy said, "and we don't have to go today if we don't want to."

"But isn't Thursday craft day?"

"Big deal. They're probably making those stupid pot holders again. I've made about 20 already this summer. What are you going to do?"

"Probably go to Academy Street School and play ball."

"What are you, nuts? It's almost 100 degrees out there. You'll die."

"You sound just like my sister," Bernie said. "You girls are so soft."

"You guys are so stupid."

"Will you please be quiet?" Marie shouted. "I'm trying to watch this movie."

At that, naturally, Mom came in and told us to be quiet because, "Mr. Mantle is on the phone."

"Mom, can Bernie and I play in my room until he's off the phone?" I knew this was normally a no-no, but I also knew Mom was a lot easier with us when she had other adults in the house.

"Go on," she said. "Just don't wrestle or play football on the bed."

We were upstairs in a flash. Bernie thought it was so great that I had my own room, because he always had to share his room with his brother. He threw himself on my bed and started going through my collection of *Superman* comics. "Do you think Mickey Mantle is allergic to Kryptonite?" he asked.

We read comics for about 15 minutes before Mickey came up to see what we were doing. "You guys ain't gonna sit in here all afternoon, are ya?"

"We were waiting for you," I said, as I jumped to attention. I didn't want him to think that I was a "lazy, good-for-nothin' bum." That was our mailman's favorite line for us when he saw us all hangin' out on Larry's front porch.

"Your sister said you guys might be up for some more baseball. Is that true?"

"We are, Mr. Mantle," Bernie said, as he got up, too. "Are you?"

"Only if I get to pitch," he said. "I need to work on my knuckle ball. Especially since I never got to play shortstop this morning." Then, he gave me a funny look.

"You got there too late," I said in self-defense. "But if we play over at the Academy Street playground, you can pitch every other inning."

"Let's go. If I can't get back to New York this afternoon, I might as well practice here. Otherwise, I'll never get back in the lineup."

When Mom realized what we were going to do, she tried to talk us out of it, saying it was much too hot.

"I don't mean to be disrespectful, ma'am," Mick said laughing, "but we'd call this a cool summer's day down in Oklahoma."

"Well, at least take some water with you, then."

"Mom," I said, not wanting to drag our thermos over there, "Timmy Sutton lives right next to the park, and we can use his hose any time."

"All right, but make sure you don't get in any trouble over there. We don't need any more phone calls from the people in that neighborhood."

"We're playing two-on-two, Ma. We never get in trouble that way."

"All right, get out of here."

When we went outside, Mick hopped on my bike again. Then, right after he got on, he got off again, looked at the clothespins clipped to the wheel frame on the front and back tires and said, "Jimbo, why do you have these here?"

"Ah, I've been meaning to put some new cards on there, and I just haven't done it yet."

"What for?"

"Here, I'll show you," Bernie said, and he pulled a bunch of baseball cards out of his back pocket. I watched as Bernie carefully skipped over the Mick's card and his other Yankee cards and put a Jerry Lumpe card on one of the clothespins near the front wheel. Then, he put the other cards back in his pocket, hopped on the bike, and rode around the back yard.

When Mick saw and heard the card flapping against the wheel's spokes, he laughed out loud and said, "Let's get some others on there, too, so we can get a real motorcycle sound."

Bernie rode over to Mick, handed him half the cards he had in his pocket — the half he didn't care about, of course — and told Mick, "Here, you choose three more to put on there."

Mick looked at the cards and talked as he made his choices. "Juan Pizarro? Nah. Bob Purkey? Nah. Bill Mazerowski! Yeah, definitely put him on that front tire. Okay, who else? Nellie Fox? Nah. Tito Francona? Nah. Hey, don't you have any Yankees here?"

"You don't want to wreck Yankee cards, do ya?" Bernie asked.

"I'll buy ya some more cards later. Let's see who ya got." Bernie handed them over.

"You're right; you don't want to wreck this one," Mick said, as he handed his own card back to Bernie. "But we do want this one on there," Mick laughed, as he picked out Joe Pepitone's card and said, "He's a real wise guy." Then, he skipped over Whitey Ford, Bobby Richardson, and Hector Lopez. "And this one, too; he's another young whippersnapper," he laughed again, as he chose pitcher Jim Bouton's card to go on the back wheel with first baseman Pepitone.

When Bernie finished clipping all the cards on to the clothespins, Mick hopped aboard again and cruised down the driveway with a big smile on his face. Bernie put the rest of his cards away, and we grabbed our gloves, bats, and balls and ran to catch up to him.

Larry was sitting on his front porch waiting for us, and he got up and joined us when we got to the corner of Wilson and Bunn Streets.

"It's me and Mick against you two," I said. "Bernie and I already decided."

"You gotta let us bat first, then."

"Yeah, yeah. No big deal."

Bunn Street was practically deserted except for Mr. O'Toole sitting in his hammock next to the laundromat and Mrs. Thayer sitting in her shaded porch across the street. Even the front porch of the fire station was empty. Usually, those guys are hangin' around outside when it's nice, but they must have been taking a snooze upstairs. While I told Larry about the delay in getting the car fixed, Mick weaved back and forth on my bike, so he wouldn't get too far ahead of us. Every once in a while, though, he'd go real fast to see how loud he could make the noise from the cards. He looked like he was having fun, just riding my bike down the street and lookin' at all the houses. Finally, he said, "How far is this place we're going to? And are there any hills?"

"It's right over there," I said, as we approached the corner of Blood Street, and I pointed to the school one block down.

Once Mick saw it, he sped ahead of us and wheeled the bike into the empty lot where we played. The lot used to be all dirt and stone, but they paved it all over, including the little hill that led up to the fence on the back side. Mickey was flying up and down the hill just like we usually did when we weren't playing ball. Once we got all set up, he came over, pretended to turn off his motorcycle, and Bernie explained the rules to him.

"Here's the strike zone marked in chalk, and the pitcher calls balls and strikes."

"That's a pretty big strike zone, isn't it?" Mick asked, looking at the marked bricks.

"Nobody likes to get a walk, Mick." Larry said.

Then, Bernie continued with the rules. "If you hit a ground ball to the hill or if a fielder drops a ground ball, it's a single. Off the hill is a double, and a dropped liner or fly ball is a double. If you hit the fence or the first floor of that factory, it's a triple, and if you hit it over the fence or hit the second floor of that factory, it's a home run."

"So, if I hit it over that fence," Mick said, pointing to the back side of Bunn Street, "are we going to get in trouble?"

"Nah," I told him. "That only happens when we play the other way with full teams and hit the ball toward those houses on Blood Street. We haven't broken a window yet playing two-on-two this way."

"And what happens if I hit it over the second floor of that factory?"

"It's three outs," Bernie said, laughing.

"No," said Mickey in disbelief.

"No," I said. "It's a home run if you hit it up there, but if it stays on the roof, we have to use another ball. If it bounces over, we just have to chase it."

"Who chases? The hitter or the pitcher?"

"The hitter," Bernie said, lying again. He was really starting to feel comfortable with Mickey.

Mick knew he was lying, though, and before Bernie could run away, Mick had him in a headlock again and was giving him noogies.

"Are you telling the truth, son?"

"Yes," Bernie said, trying to wiggle free. But after a few more noogies, he gave up and said, "All right, I give up. I'm lying."

"Do you promise to chase every ball I hit over the fence off you this afternoon?" Two more noogies.

"I promise."

"Cross your heart and hope to die?" One more noogie. Larry and I were both laughing like crazy.

"Cross my heart and hope to die."

"Who's your favorite ballplayer?" Mick said, just as he was about to let him go.

"Roger Maris," Bernie answered, thinking he could get away. Bernie's not too smart sometimes. Or very quick. Mick had him back in a headlock in no time and started with the noogies all over again.

"I'm just kiddin', Mick," Bernie said, trying to cover up his head. "You're my favorite, and seven's my favorite number."

"All right, all right. Let's get started," Mick said, as he finally let Bernie go. He grabbed Dad's glove off the handlebars of my bike, and I showed him the spot where he had to pitch from.

"How many warmups do I get?"

"Take as many as you need," Larry said. Mick probably thought Larry was being nice, but I could tell Larry wanted to check him out before he had to hit against him. He stood next to the batter's box and tried to time Mick's pitches as they came in.

I stood next to Mick and watched him throw. He was moaning and groaning as he loosened up. Part of it was an act, I could tell, but part of it was real, too. He didn't look as smooth or as strong throwing the ball as he did hitting it. It looked kinda like his muscles were getting in the way of each other when he pitched. I could tell his left foot was still bothering him, too, because he didn't use much of a windup, and he made a little face every time he let go of the ball, and all his weight was on that leg.

"How come we're using rubber balls?" he asked, after about four or five pitches.

"Hard balls get eaten up too fast on the brick wall and the asphalt, and the rubber balls only cost a quarter."

"I don't know if my knuckler's going to work," he said. "Here goes." The ball practically disappeared in his hand and then fluttered up to the wall when he threw.

"Oh, baby," Larry said, licking his chops. "I'm going downtown if you throw that softee up here."

Mickey just laughed at him. "Yeah, that's what Joe Pepitone said when he first saw it, but he still can't hit it, and he's been trying like crazy."

"It's not as good as with a hardball," he whispered to me, "but those two knuckleheads won't be able to hit it."

Finally, we got started, and Mickey threw the first pitch right at Larry's head. He didn't throw it that hard, so Larry got out of the way no problem, but then Mick yelled, "Strike one," even though the pitch was two feet inside.

"You gotta be kiddin'," Larry yelled back at him.

"Pitcher calls balls and strikes, and 'nobody likes to get a walk.' You said so yourself." I think Mickey was testing Larry.

"Yeah, that's the only way you'll strike me out anyway is by making bad calls."

Mickey laughed again. Then, he threw a fastball for a real strike, and Larry lined it right back at Mick. He caught it easily and then turned and threw it to me like he was throwing it around the horn. "One down, Jimbo! Stay alive out there."

When Bernie stepped in to hit next, Mickey tested him, too. "Okay, Bernie Boy, tell me again who chases it if somebody hits a home run. The hitter or the pitcher?"

"The pitcher," Bernie said, getting it right this time.

"All right," Mick said. "Just checking. Not that I have to worry about you hitting a home run off me."

Actually, what he said was true. Bernie usually didn't hit many home runs, but he was digging in as if he meant to hit at least one today. He definitely wanted to get even for all those noogies.

Mickey threw Bernie a knuckle ball for a strike, and Bernie just looked at it. Then, he threw him another one, and Bernie swung and missed by a mile. On the third pitch, Bernie was waiting for the knuckler, and Mickey blew a fastball by him for strike three.

"He crossed him up with the fastball," Mick said in his best Mel Allen imitation. Then, he fielded the ball as it rolled back to him from the wall and turned to throw it to me again. Instead of chattering this time, though, Mick kept announcing the game for us. "Two down here in the top of the first, and it looks like Mantle's got his best stuff working for him. If he can get his curve ball over the plate, too, he'll be tough to beat today."

Larry stepped in again and begged Mickey to throw him that slow knuckler.

"I'll throw it when you least expect it," Mick said, and he threw Larry his curve ball. Larry popped it up to me for an easy out, and we switched sides.

"You bat first," I said to Mick, trying to be polite.

"Nope. Pitcher always bats last," he said. "You go ahead."

Larry was warming up and throwing as hard as he could, like he always did. Larry was a great pitcher at Academy Street because the strike zone was so big. In Little League, though, Larry was too wild. His manager let Larry pitch once, and he walked the first five batters he faced and hit the sixth. That was the end of his Little League pitching career.

When I stepped in to hit against Larry, he threw his first pitch right at my head and called, "Strike one."

"Gee, I wonder where he learned that," Mick said to me. "C'mon, Jimbo, hit one back at him and knock his block off."

I tried on the next pitch, but I didn't hit it very hard. I hit a weak grounder past Larry that Bernie caught easily for the first out. When Mick stepped in to hit, he started complaining about the bats again.

"Where's that Mickey Mantle bat I used this morning?"

"It was Omeo's, and he brought it home with him."

"Would you go get it for me?"

I knew he was testing me, too, so I said, "Okay," and pretended to go toward my bike.

"Get back here, Jimbo. There's gotta be at least one decent bat here. Let's see, Ted Kluszewski, Stan Musial, Frank Robinson, or Harmon Killebrew? Let's try Kluszewski." Then, he rolled up the sleeves on his shirt just like Kluszewski, and he stepped in to hit.

Larry started his windup and threw his first pitch right down the middle for a called "Strike one." I think Mick was surprised to see a 12-year-old kid throw the ball as hard as Larry did, but he didn't realize Larry was cheatin'. If you didn't keep an eye on Larry, he'd take a few steps forward and then start his windup, so that by the time he let go of the ball, he was right on top of you, and he was unhittable. If I were hitting, I would have said something and made Larry start over again. Since Mick was a lot older than we were, though, and a lot bigger and stronger, I wanted to see if he'd be able to hit off Larry when he was that close and throwin' that hard, so I kept my mouth shut.

Larry fired two more hard ones from in close, and both were outside the strike zone. By the time he threw another strike, Mick was ready. He crushed the next pitch and hit a line drive that bounced off the wall of the factory just below the roof for a home run.

"One nothing, good guys," he yelled at Larry, and then he asked Bernie, "What number is that, Bernie Boy?"

"418," Bernie yelled back.

As I watched Mickey, I couldn't believe how excited he was getting. When he hits home runs on television, he jogs around the bases with his head down and doesn't seem to be excited at all. But after his two home runs this morning and his first one this afternoon, he was all pumped up like it was the last game of the World Series. Maybe he was just feelin' good about playin' again after being injured for so long.

When I stepped in to hit again, I told Larry to stay by the line for the pitcher's mound, which was even with the street light outside the fence. Since there was no actual mound, it was hard for the batter to see if the pitcher was really standing where he was supposed to be, especially in Larry's case. I think he moved back to where he was supposed to be, but I couldn't be sure.

Anyway, I hit another grounder to Bernie for the second out, Mick hit a triple off the fence, and I popped up for the third out. Though we were ahead 1-0 as we switched sides again for the top of the second, I felt terrible, because I had made all three outs. Some future Yankee centerfielder I was. And things only got worse.

During the next couple of innings, I was making most of the outs for our team, and Larry and Bernie were hitting me pretty hard when it was my turn to pitch. We were still winning, of course, by about 15 to 8, because Mickey was hitting mostly triples and homers, but I hadn't even come close to the fence. Then, during the bottom of the fifth, Mickey put our last ball up on the roof of the factory, and he gave Bernie a dollar bill to buy four more balls. He also gave Larry a dollar bill to buy some sodas for us, so the two of them took the money and headed off to Stahl's Corner Store on the top of Wall Street in front of the school.

While Mickey and I sat in the shade of the school and waited for them, Mickey started givin' me a hard time, but he wasn't foolin' around.

"How come you don't swing hard when you bat?"

"Ah, I just can't seem to get a solid hit today, even when Bernie pitches," I said, trying to make myself feel better.

"No, I'm not talkin' about the way you hit the ball; I'm talkin' about the way you swing. You don't swing hard at all."

"Well, I don't want to swing and miss."

"Why not?"

"I might strike out."

"So what?"

"So, I hate it when *you* strike out."

"You hate it when *I* strike out? How do you think I feel?"

"So why do you do it?"

"You think I strike out on purpose?"

"No, but I think you could at least hit the ball every time if you wanted."

"What's so great about hittin' the ball every time?"

"Well, at least then you have a chance of getting on base. You might get a hit, or they might make an error. But if you strike out, you don't do anything for the team."

"So that's why you don't swing hard?"

"I don't want to strike out."

"Have you ever struck out?"

"Yeah."

"And?"

"And I hate it."

"So you hate it when you strike out, too; not just when I strike out."

"Yep."

"What about when Larry and Bernie strike out?"

"I don't like it when they're on my team."

"You're a good team player, Jimbo. I can see that. But you gotta stop worrying about striking out so much, or you're never going to hit a home run."

"What's hitting a home run got to do with striking out?"

"Everything. If you keep takin' that baby swing of yours when you hit, all you're ever gonna get is singles and a few doubles if you're lucky. Have you hit any triples yet this year?"

"Yeah, I got one."

"Let me guess. You hit a pop-fly to right, the rightfielder misjudged it, and you got three bases."

I hated to admit it, but he was exactly right. I was so proud of that triple because it was the closest I'd ever come to a home run in a Little League game. If Ed Krehl knew how to play baseball, though, it would have been an easy out.

"Tell ya what, Jimbo. Here's what I want you to do. When Larry and Bernie get back and we start playin' again, I want you to swing as hard as you can at every pitch."

"Even when I got two strikes on me?"

"Even when you got two strikes on you."

"I'll probably strike out."

"Of course you're going to strike out. You might strike out a lot at first. But guess what?"

"What?"

"You're going to start hitting some home runs, too."

"Really?"

"Jimbo, you already know how to hit the ball. Now you gotta learn how to hit it hard. But you ain't gonna hit it hard if you don't try. And guess what else?"

"What?"

"If you strike out, it's only one out. It's not three outs. It's not the end of the world. And every time you strike out brings you that much closer to hitting a home run."

"Really?"

"Believe me. I know all about striking out and hitting home runs. You can trust me on this one."

"I'll do it on one condition," I said.

"What's that?"

"When you get back to the Yankees, you promise not to strike out so much."

"I told you, I don't strike out on purpose."

"Yeah, but you probably try and hit it 600 feet every time when all you need to do is hit it 400 or 450 for a home run."

"So what exactly do you want me to do?"

"Just hit the ball. Don't try and kill it every time you swing, so you swing and miss and strike out."

"That won't be easy for me, but I'll tell ya what I'll do."

"What."

"If you promise to swing harder this afternoon, then the first time I bat again in a real game, I'll just try to meet the ball. I won't try to kill it. I promise."

"You got a deal," I said, and we shook hands on it, just seconds before Bernie and Larry returned with the new balls and the sodas.

"What took you guys so long?" Mick asked.

"Bernie couldn't decide between grape and cola."

"So whatd'ya finally get?"

"Root beer."

While we were drinking the sodas, Larry asked Mick why he was driving near Amsterdam when his car broke down.

"You mean to tell me you guys haven't figured that out yet?"

"You were lost," Bernie said.

"No, I wasn't lost."

"You were scouting minor leaguers up in Syracuse or Buffalo?" I guessed.

"Wrong again."

"I'll give you a hint. There's a famous tourist attraction up near here that I came to visit."

"Oh, I know now," Bernie said excitedly. "Howe Caverns."

Mickey laughed at that one. So did Larry and I. Then, Mick said, "Ya know, sometimes, those city slickers down in the Bronx say you guys upstate are a bunch of country bumpkins, and I'm starting to think they might be right."

"I ain't no bumpkin," Larry said, as if he were really offended, "but I don't think you came up here to see the Auriesville Shrine."

"What about you, Jimbo. I'll give you one more guess."

I thought it over again and wondered why would Mickey Mantle travel up the Thruway from New York City while he was on the injured list and not able to play?

"I know," I said finally, not wanting to believe that I hadn't thought of it sooner. "You went to the Baseball Hall of Fame in Cooperstown."

"Congratulations. You have correctly answered the $64,000 question."

"You went up there by yourself?" Bernie asked, as if he thought Mickey were lying.

"Yeah, Ralph told me to take a day off and not come to the ballpark. He said having me there but not being able to play me was driving him nuts. So, I took his advice and took a drive up to Cooperstown to see what the Hall of Fame was really like."

"You mean to tell me," Larry jumped in, "you'd never been to Cooperstown?"

"Oh, I was there before. In fact, I hit a home run at Doubleday Field down the street in 1954 in an exhibition game, but they rushed us in and out of there so fast, I didn't get to see anything. Yesterday, I took my sweet time and really enjoyed it."

"Did you see the rug?" I asked.

"Yeah, there were lots of rugs up there. They were all over the place. What rug? What are you talking about?"

"Amsterdam's got a little piece of a rug up there that says, 'Amsterdam Welcomes the New York Yankees.'"

"It's in the Hall of Fame?"

"Yeah, it's in a frame on the wall, in the basement, I think, near the back staircase."

"I didn't see it."

"Did you see that set of four pictures of you and Hank Bauer bobbling a ball in right field?"

"Yeah, wasn't that a great set of photos! I remember that play like it happened yesterday. The whole thing seemed like it was in slow motion."

"The rug was on the wall on the other side. Are you sure you didn't see it?"

"I didn't see it, Jimbo. I'm sorry. I promise to look for it the next time I'm up there."

"Hey, wait a minute." Larry said. "Why were you on 5-S instead of the Thruway? You should have gotten on the Thruway in Canajoharie if you were comin' back from Cooperstown."

Mick looked at Larry, then he looked at Bernie and me, and said, "This boy is not a country bumpkin."

"So what happened?" Larry asked, determined to get his answer.

"I don't know what happened exactly, but there must have been some kind of accident on the Thruway, because they made all the cars going east get off the Thruway at Exit 28 and detour down 5-S to Exit 27. And it was on 5-S, your Honor, not too far from the Thruway, that my car broke down. Cross my heart and hope to die."

We all laughed some more, and then Bernie asked, "So, Mick, do you think you'll make the Hall of Fame someday?"

Mick actually seemed to get a little embarrassed, like he wasn't sure if he was good enough, so Larry answered the question for him.

"Of course he's going to be in the Hall of Fame. What kind of stupid question is that?"

"Yeah," I added, "and it will be the first time a guy who was named after a Hall of Famer makes it to the Hall of Fame himself."

"That's right, Jimbo. How'd you know that?"

"I read a book about you. It said your dad named you after Mickey Cochrane, the old catcher for the Detroit Tigers."

"Right again, Jimbo, which reminds me. Your dad said you'd tell me the story behind why they call you 'Jimbo.'"

"It's not 'Jimbo,'" Bernie said. "It's Jumbo, like the elephant."

"It is? I'm sorry, Jimbo; I mean, Jumbo."

"Yeah, and he got that name," Larry added, "because his ears are so big."

"That's not true," I said, defending myself. "They call me 'Jumbo' at school because I'm taller than everybody else, especially these two little pipsqueaks."

"Yeah," Larry laughed, "well, these two little pipsqueaks are makin' you look pretty bad today. If you didn't have this Hall of Famer on your side, we'd be killin' ya."

"C'mon," I said. "Let's go, right now. I want to show Mick how far those rubber balls travel when they're new."

Within seconds, we all finished our sodas and were playing again. Larry was pitching, and he blew the ball by me three times for strikes, not because he was throwing that great, but because I was swinging hard, just like Mick told me to do. I couldn't quite seem to keep my eye on the ball and swing real hard at the same time. I was tempted to let up just a little bit the next time I was up, but Mick kept tellin' me to swing real hard, to try and hit the ball up on the factory roof like he had done. I didn't come close. I hit a little dribbler back to Larry for the second out, and I struck out again for the third out, while Mick kept hittin' line drives off the fence and the factory.

During the last four innings, I started to make a little progress. I was hitting hard line drives instead of ground balls and easy pop-ups, and I was even pitchin' better when it was my turn. Just before I began to pitch the sixth inning, Mick came up to me and whispered, "You know, you should be trying to throw the ball a lot harder when you pitch, too."

"But I'll probably start walkin' these guys," I said automatically.

"So what." Mickey said again, just like he had done before, and I knew exactly what he meant. I might walk more batters, but I might also strike out more batters if I threw the ball harder, if I really put all of my energy into every pitch instead of trying to be so perfect every time.

By the time the game was over and we started to head home, I still hadn't hit any home runs, but, just like Mickey said, I could feel like I was getting closer. And in the bottom of the eighth, the last inning I pitched, I struck out the side; I got Larry once and Bernie twice. They asked me about it, too, as we walked up Blood Street and down Bunn.

"What was that pitch you were throwing us at the end?"

"Just a fastball."

"No," Larry said. "It was more than a fastball. It had a little hop to it."

"It was a cut fastball," Mickey jumped in, as if he were trying to keep our private conversation a secret. "I taught it to him. It's the same one Whitey Ford throws when he really needs a strikeout."

"Show me, too," Bernie said.

"Catch me, and I'll show you," Mickey said laughing, and he rode off toward Wilson Avenue with Bernie chasing after him.

"So he never told you how to hit home runs, did he?" Larry asked. I guess he hadn't noticed how much harder I was hittin' the ball toward the end.

"Nah," I lied. "He was so psyched up about pitchin' and throwin' his knuckle balls and curve balls that I think he forgot all about giving batting tips."

"Too bad."

"Yeah, too bad."

When we got to the corner of Bunn Street and Henry Street, Bernie and Mick were waiting for us outside Rudy's Corner Store. "C'mon," Mick said. "I promised Bernie I'd buy him some baseball cards."

Bernie led the way as we walked down the stairs on the side of Rudy's house to his small basement store. Inside, the air conditioner was humming, and I actually felt a chill as I walked in from the 100-degree heat outside. No wonder the Fetterly brothers were so anxious earlier to get back to their air-conditioned living room.

We weren't at all surprised to find the store empty, but Mick was pretty puzzled about it. "Where's Rudy?" he asked.

"Ah, he usually takes a nap upstairs," Larry answered. "He's gotta be 80 years old."

"So how do we call him?"

"We don't," Bernie said. "We just take what we want and leave our money here on the counter. Look, somebody left a quarter. They must have come in for a loaf of bread." Then, Bernie started looking at the baseball cards as if he could see through the wrappers.

"How many can I get, Mick?"

Mick flipped Bernie a quarter and said, "Here, get five packs, and make sure I get a piece of that gum. You guys want any cards?" he said to Larry and me.

"Sure," Larry said, and I crowded in behind him. Mick put two more quarters on the counter, and Larry and I each took five packs, too.

After he got a piece of gum from Bernie, Mick sat down in Rudy's rocker and tried to blow bubbles, while the three of us went through our cards.

"Got 'em. Got 'em. Don't got 'em. Got 'em. Don't got 'em." It would have been so neat if one of us got a Mickey Mantle card while he was sittin' there with us, but it didn't happen. Bernie was happy to get the Yankee team card and a checklist for the fifth series in his cards, and Larry was upset because he got three New York Mets. The only Yankee I got was Johnny Blanchard.

We were all so relaxed just leaning up against the counter and the soda coolers, checking out our cards, that we were surprised to hear the door open and see Mike Savarese, the Ward Alderman, walk in. "Hi ya, boys," he said, without really looking at us. "Hot enough for ya?" He quickly grabbed two Nehi orange sodas out of the first cooler, put his two dimes on the counter, and started back out. Then, he turned back and looked straight at Mickey sitting in Rudy's rocker, reached out his hand to him, and said, "Don't believe we've met. My name's Mike Savarese. Are you new to the neighborhood?"

Mick stood up to shake hands. "Just visiting, actually. I'll be leaving tonight."

"What's your name?"

"Mick. Mickey Mantle."

"Pleased to meet you, Mick," Mike said. "Stop by any time." And he left as quickly as he came in.

"People just do this?" Mick asked. "Come in, grab what they need, and leave their money?"

"Or they hang around and wait for Rudy to come back, like we're doin'," Bernie answered.

"What if they don't have the right change?"

Larry answered next. "When that happens to me, I usually just give him the money the next time I'm here."

"I suppose you never forget, either?"

"That might happen once in a while," Larry admitted with a laugh, "but I never do it on purpose. Rudy's my friend."

Then, I asked Mick, "You don't have places like this in Oklahoma?"

"Oh, we have storekeepers who fall asleep, but they usually do it in the store, so all you have to do is wake them up. They don't sleep upstairs and leave the store empty."

After another few minutes of just hangin' around, Mick got up and said, "We better get goin', guys. Doesn't look like Rudy will be back any time soon." He started for the door, but then he stopped before going out. "Are you sure we left enough money for all those baseball cards?"

"We each got five packs, Mick, and they're only a nickel each. We're okay."

"All right. Let's go, then."

At Larry's house, Larry's dad was just getting home from work. He still had his hard hat on, and he was just pullin' his bag of tools out of the back of his friend's pickup truck.

"What are you guys up to?" he asked, though he was sayin' good-by to his buddy at the same time.

"Dad, this is Mickey Mantle," Larry said excitedly.

"I'm sure it is," his dad said, not quite believing and squinting through his thick glasses to try and find out for sure.

"Your son's sure got a mean fastball," Mick said, as he reached out to shake hands.

"He didn't hurt anybody with it, did he?"

"Only when he struck me out," Mick answered. Larry got him with a change-up in the last inning, the only change-up he'd thrown all day.

"You struck out Mickey Mantle? I don't believe it." And I couldn't tell if he doubted it was really Mickey Mantle or if he doubted that Larry really struck him out.

"No, it really happened," Mick admitted. "Your son could be the next Ryne Duren."

We all laughed at that one because we always kidded Larry that he was Ryne Duren, the former Yankee reliever who scared most batters because his milk-bottle lenses made it look like he couldn't see and because he was so wild and so fast when he pitched.

While we were laughing about that, Mick started asking Larry's dad about his tools and his job as a roofer and sheet-metal worker. I knew Mick had worked in the coal mines of Oklahoma before he became a Yankee, and I wondered what he would do for a living after he retired from baseball. Maybe he'd be a manager or a coach like so many other old ballplayers. Or maybe he'd be an announcer, and he'd get to introduce me when I finally made it to the Major Leagues.

Bernie brought me back from my daydream when he nudged me and showed me my dad's car approaching. Dad slowed down as he turned the corner and yelled to Larry's dad, "Hey, Don, send those guys home, will ya?"

"Is my car fixed?" Mick yelled back.

"Just about. Let's go," and he drove up Wilson Avenue to our house.

Mick said good-by and shook hands with Larry and Larry's dad, and then he rode my bike home, while Bernie and I ran after him. Dad was waiting for us in the driveway. At the house, Mick shook Bernie's hand and said good-by to him, but Bernie wasn't quite ready to let him go.

"Will you do one favor for me before you leave?"

"What's that, Bernie Boy?"

"Will you sign my baseball card?" And he pulled it out of his back pocket again.

"No problem."

I had to laugh a little while Mick was signing Bernie's card with my dad's pen, because Bernie had always made fun of people who collected autographs. "What good is an autograph," he always said, "unless it's on a check?"

When we went in the house, we could smell the spaghetti sauce and meatballs Mom had made for supper. While we were washing our hands, I heard Dad tell Mickey about the car.

"I stopped at Natale's after work, and the final parts had just arrived from Albany. Frank said the car would be all set within an hour, so you might as well eat first and then hit the road."

During supper, Dad asked Mick what he had done all day, so Mick told him about our come-from-behind victory this morning at the Cage and about his pitching this afternoon at Academy.

"That was awful nice of you to play with the boys all day, Mr. Mantle," Mom told him.

"Are you kiddin'?" he told her. "I love playin' ball, especially when I'm healthy, and this leg is just about ready for Yankee Stadium again. I can't wait to get back in the lineup."

"Did you learn anything from him today?" Dad asked me.

"Yeah, but it's top secret," I said smiling at Mick. "You'll have to wait until tonight's game to see."

I couldn't wait to play again myself. After startin' to hit those rubber balls hard that afternoon, I felt like I could do the same thing with the hard balls that night. After supper, I hustled upstairs to get my Slezak's uniform on, and Mick changed back into his good clothes.

While I was getting dressed, I rolled my uniform sleeves up to my shoulders just like Ted Kluszewski always did and just like Mick did this afternoon. It didn't have the same effect for me. My skinny, little arms looked a lot better all covered up.

Before I went back downstairs, I grabbed the Mantle and Maris book I bought up in Cooperstown, the book commemorating Roger's 61 homers and Mick's 54 in 1961. I had never asked for an autograph before either, but, like Bernie, I wanted some kind of proof that Mickey Mantle had really spent the day with me in Amsterdam. I was afraid I'd wake up and find out the whole thing was a dream. Dad had an even better idea.

He had pulled out his camera and he took a picture of Mick signing the book for me, and then he took pictures of the two of us sitting on the back steps and standing in the back yard.

Before he left with Dad to go get his car and head back to New York City, Mick kissed each of the girls and Mom, and he shook my hand and gave me a hug, too. As he did, he whispered in my ear, "Don't forget to swing hard tonight. And don't go back to that baby swing of yours if you strike out once or twice."

"Okay," I said quietly. I felt like I was about to cry, now that he was really getting ready to go. It had been the best day of my life.

"And don't forget to come down and see a game later this summer," he said, as he hopped in the front seat of our car. "I'll take care of the tickets." Then, he was gone.

Chapter Four

Two minutes after Mick left, Billy Whelly's mom pulled in the driveway to give me a ride to our game against Nadler's Dairy.

"What'd you do today?" Billy asked, as I climbed in the back seat.

"You wouldn't believe it if I told you," I said, suddenly exhausted and not quite ready to tell the whole story yet.

"Yeah, well you're not going to believe what happened to me either." Then, I sat back and listened all the way to Isabel's Field, while he told me about his new bike with the banana seat and the high handlebars and how he almost killed himself trying to learn how to do wheelies.

During batting practice before the game, I was hitting the ball great. Coach wasn't throwing hard, of course, so it was pretty easy, but he noticed something.

"What'd you have for supper, Slugger?" he asked.

"Spaghetti and meatballs."

"Well, save some of that power for the game, will ya?"

On my last three swings, I tried to reach the left-field fence, and I failed miserably. Instead of the hard line drives I had been hitting, I hit three weak grounders to the infield.

"You're pulling your head out too soon," Coach yelled at me. "Keep your eye on the ball. Take one more good swing and get out of there."

On the next pitch, I swung as hard as I could and I kept my eye on the ball, and I actually hit one over the fence — foul.

"Straighten that baby out, Jumbo, and you'll be trottin' around the bases tonight." I was so psyched.

During my first time up in the bottom of the first inning, I was too psyched. I swung at a bad pitch that was way outside the strike zone and hit a routine grounder to shortstop.

Then, in the third inning, I got up with the score tied at two and the bases loaded. By then, my whole family had arrived, and they were sitting in the stands behind the first-base dugout eating Snow Cones. I was thinking grand slam and a 6-2 lead. The count went to three and two, as I fouled off two line drives over the third-base dugout. The payoff pitch was way over my head, but I was so anxious to hit that I swung and didn't even come close. I went down swinging for the third out of the inning.

As I was throwing ground balls to the other infielders before the top of the fourth, I felt like a piece of crap. I was so determined to hit my first home run, and a grand slam home run at that, that I'd forgotten about trying to knock in some runs and win the game. If I had let that last pitch go, I would have walked to first base, and we would have had a 3-2 lead.

"You're a good team player, Jimbo; I can see that." That's what Mick had said about me earlier that day, though I didn't feel like it was true any more. "Gotta get my head back in this ball game," I told myself.

By the time I got to bat in the bottom of the fifth, we were ahead 5-2, and it looked like it would be my last time up. With two outs and nobody on, I could swing for the fence if I wanted to, and it wouldn't matter to anybody. We'd get them out in the top of the sixth — Jeff Baker was pitching a great game after giving up two runs early — and go home with our fourth straight win. But I knew if I swung for the fence, I'd probably hit a weak grounder just like I did in batting practice. So, as I circled behind the catcher and the umpire and stepped into the batter's box, I made up my mind to get a good pitch to hit, swing hard at it, and see what happened.

The first pitch was high, so I let it go. Billy Dado obviously remembered how he had struck me out on that pitch the last time up, and he decided to try it again.

The next two pitches were curve balls outside, so the count was 3-0. Coach never let us swing on 3-0, and Billy Dado knew it, too, and fired a strike. The 3-1 pitch was the pitch I'd been waiting for, a strike right down the middle of the plate, about waist high. I swung as hard as I could and made good contact, but I got under it a bit too much. It was a high fly to left center. I put my head down and ran as hard as I could, even though I knew it was a sure out. If I was going to be oh-for-three for the night, I had to at least hustle a little bit. When I got halfway to second and looked up, I saw an amazing thing. The leftfielder and the centerfielder came together at the fence near the sign for Mac's Confectionary, and neither one of them was able to catch the ball. My high pop-fly had carried far enough to clear the green, wooden fence by a good ten feet. It wasn't even close.

I was so excited, I didn't even remember to trot the rest of the way. I sprinted to third, got a handshake, a big smile, and an "Attaboy" from Coach Gorman, and cruised on home. There, the rest of the team had already gathered to congratulate me. My first ever home run in Little League wasn't the game-winner I'd always imagined, and I hadn't even realized that it might go out, but I didn't care about any of that. I just felt so proud when I trotted back to the dugout and saw my family and Mick cheering for me.

Mick? What was he doing here? He was supposed to be on his way back to New York City.

"Way to go, Jumbo Jimbo," he said, as he came to the fence near the dugout, shook my hand, and slapped me on the back. "I had a feeling you might get one tonight, and I didn't want to miss it. Gotta go now, though, so take it easy. Thanks for everything."

I was speechless. How long had he been there? Did he see me strike out, too? Did he really think I was going to hit one out? How did he know?

I don't even know what happened in the top of the sixth except that we got three outs somehow and won the game. Between pitches of that inning, I just kept looking out at the left-field fence where my home run had gone over. Then, I tried to remember what had happened to the ball. Did somebody chase after it and throw it back in? Or, did someone grab it and run off with it? Would I be able to get it somehow and have my picture taken with it like Mick always did when he hit a special one, like the tape-measure home-run he hit off Chuck Stobbs, or the one he hit for home-run number 300, or the grand slam he hit in the 1954 World Series?

On the way home in the car, the girls were fighting over some keychains a politician had handed out in the park during the game, and Mom and Dad were trying to decide if they needed to stop at the grocery store on the way home. I wanted to talk about my first home run, but nobody was all that interested.

When we got to Joe's Market, Dad let Mom and the girls go in to get what we needed, and he and I sat in the front seat of the car.

"I bet it felt pretty good, huh?" he said.

"Ya know, Dad, I didn't even think it was going to be that close to the fence. I thought it was just going to be an easy out."

"Once you hit a few more, you'll probably get used to the feel of it."

"Did you ever hit one, Dad?"

He looked at me like that was the dumbest question I'd ever asked in my life.

"You've seen me hit home runs in softball, haven't you?"

"Softball doesn't count, Dad. That's for old guys."

I knew I was in trouble as soon as I said it. He reached over, got me in a bear hug, and started tickling me and teasing me at the same time.

"So now you're a big home-run hitter, a big star, a hot shot."

"I'm sorry, Dad. I was only kidding. Softball's a great game." Fortunately, he let me off easy, probably because we were in the car.

"So, Dad, do you think we can go to Yankee Stadium before the end of the season? Mick said he'd get us free tickets."

"Sure, we'll go down."

"When?"

"Well, you'll probably want to wait until he's off the disabled list and able to play a whole game."

"Yeah. How about when they play the White Sox?"

"When's that?"

"I got the whole schedule on the back of my bedroom door. I'll check it out as soon as we get home."

"All right."

We were both quiet for a few seconds. Then, Dad asked, "So, you had a good time with him?"

"Definitely. I couldn't believe he stayed around for the game tonight. Did you ask him to?"

"No. I was as surprised as you were. I waited at Natale's until the car was all set to go, and I showed him how to get back on the Thruway, but at the corner of Market and Main, he pulled over and told me he wanted to see your game before he left. So, he followed me back to the house to get Mom and the girls, and then we all went to the game."

"When did you get there? Did he see me strike out in the third?"

"He did. We got there in the top half of the inning, but he didn't want you to know he was there, so he sat in his car down the first-base line a little bit. Good thing, too, because he probably would have been mobbed by the crowd if they knew he was there."

"Dad, did you know it was Mickey Mantle when we first stopped to help him with his car?"

"No."

"When did you know for sure who it was?"

"I knew for sure when I got close to him and saw his face and his arms and his neck. I always thought your Uncle Tony had the strongest arms I'd ever seen, but Mick's arms are even bigger."

"So you'd never seen him in person before?"

"No, but I've seen his face in the paper a million times. And I saw that look on your face, too, when you realized we weren't going to be able to get his car fixed right away."

"No offense, Dad, but I was kinda hopin' you couldn't fix it."

"It's all right. I enjoyed having him here, too."

"I think he had a good time; don't you?"

"As a matter of fact, on the way down to pick up his car, he thanked me over and over again and told me how much he enjoyed playing ball with you guys. He even said the game at Academy Street School with just you, Larry, and Bernie reminded him of the games he played with his father and grandfather when he was a kid. He said he played with them every night after they got home from work, and that's how he learned to be a switch-hitter. Did he teach you how to bat left-handed?

"No, but maybe I'll give it a try now that I'm a home-run hitter." We both laughed again, and, just then, Mom and the girls came out of the store with the groceries.

Dad got out of the car and opened the trunk, so they could put the groceries in. I opened the passenger door to the front seat, so Mom could slide in next to Dad. As we drove down Bunn Street for home, the best day of my life was just about over. Or so I thought.

The best day of my life actually went on for some time. On the weekend after Mickey Mantle Day in Amsterdam, I became an even bigger fan of the Mick and the Yankees. I listened to the Friday-night game on the radio, and I watched the Saturday and Sunday games on TV, anxiously waiting to see how Mick would do once he got back in the lineup. By the end of Sunday's first game, though, it was pretty obvious that he wasn't ready to play full-time yet. Mel Allen announced that Mick was finally off the disabled list and that he might be able to pinch hit, but that was about it. So, when Bernie stopped by to say that he and Larry were going down to the August Festival, I asked Mom if I could go with them. I knew she'd probably say "Yes" because Dad was already down there, working as the announcer in the poker booth.

"You can go down there with them," she said, "but I want you to come right home with your father as soon as everything's over."

Once I had her okay, I raced upstairs to get a few dollars out of my bank, and, then, Bernie and I picked up Larry, and we started walking across Bunn Street toward Market Street.

The August Festival at St. Mary's Church was a big treat in Amsterdam because they set up games and food booths, and they even brought in some rides, like a merry-go-round for the little kids and a small ferris wheel for us bigger kids. Everybody showed up at some point during the Festival, and some kids were there for the entire four days from Thursday through Sunday.

Bernie and Larry and I had already been there on Friday and Saturday, but we wanted to go again just so we wouldn't miss any of the excitement.

"Did you hear Mickey Mantle came off the disabled list?" Bernie asked, as we walked past the corner of Blood Street and saw the Academy Street school down below.

"Yeah, but after I struck him out the other day," Larry said, "he's probably not quite ready for big-league pitching yet."

"He struck out on purpose against you," I said, "just to make you feel good."

"Oh, and did he tell you that right before, or after, he showed you how to hit home runs, Mr. Babe Ruth?"

We gave each other grief all the way across Bunn Street and down Market Street and were having a great time. Usually, Sundays were dead in Amsterdam because all the stores were closed, but, because of the Festival, a lot of people were on the streets heading downtown.

When we turned at the corner of Market and Main, I saw my Uncle Harry outside Brownie's Lunch again, so I asked him about Wednesday's number.

"Wednesday?" he asked, like I had lost my mind. "That's almost a week ago. Why do you want Wednesday's number?"

"I want to know if Mickey Mantle's number came in."

"What'd he play again? Do you remember?" he asked, as he searched through his little black book of numbers and notes.

"His uniform number: seven."

"Seven. That's right. No, that number hasn't come in, in a long time, and everybody plays it because of Mick, especially these last couple of years."

I didn't know that much about the numbers, but I knew Uncle Harry was right about more people liking Mickey Mantle. When I first started following Mickey's career, a lot of the guys on Dad's softball team didn't like Mick. They said he struck out too much and was too much of a hothead. But, since Mick got hurt at the end of 1961, when he was trying to beat Babe Ruth's record of 60 home runs, the older guys started liking him more. I think they felt sorry for him, especially when Roger Maris went on to hit 61 home runs and break the record. And now that Mick was hurt again after his great year last year, it seemed like everybody was rootin' for him to get healthy and start playin' like he used to.

Before we left Uncle Harry, he asked me to give him a lucky number he could play for himself. "Anything but seven," he said. "We can't afford for that number to come in."

"How 'bout 777?" I said, figuring that number was three times as good.

"You got it, Jumbo," and he wrote it down in his book. As we were walking away, Larry asked me if Uncle Harry ever let me play a number.

"No," I told him. "Besides, I'm not interested. I'd rather buy a couple hot dogs and a soda any day."

When we walked by Sears and Roebuck, they had a TV on in the window, and the second game of the doubleheader was just starting. The Yankee lineup was on the screen, but Mick's name wasn't listed.

"Still on the bench," Larry said. "I'm tellin' you, he'll probably be up here in Amsterdam again tomorrow just beggin' me to pitch against him. He knows he won't really be ready unless he can get by me first."

Bernie and I ignored Larry this time because we were so close to the Festival. We could smell the popcorn and the pizza, and we could see a lot of people gathered around the food booth for supper. I ran over to the poker booth to let Dad know that I was there and that I was riding home with him.

"All right," he said loudly through his microphone, as if he were talking only to me, but he was talking to me and to all the poker players gathered around his booth. "All right, get your quarters down. You can't win if you don't get your quarters down."

When I found Larry and Bernie again, they were helping Father Berry run the basketball booth, so I asked Coach Holland if he needed any help at the baseball booth.

"Sure, Jumbo. You can set up those wooden milk bottles for me after these people try to knock them down."

One of the best things about working at the Festival was that you got free food. The nuns came by just about every hour to see if the workers needed anything, so I was always eating while I worked: a hamburger one hour, french fries the next, and a Snow Cone or cotton candy after that. The baseball booth was great, too, because everybody in Little League stopped by to see if they could knock down the six wooden milk bottles with one ball to win a Yankee Yearbook or with two balls to win a pack of baseball cards. Mike Kachan was just about to throw when I heard my name announced over the public-address system from the poker booth. "Jim LaBate, please report to the poker booth. Jim LaBate, please report to the poker booth — now."

"Gotta go, Coach," I said as I raced off, trying to figure out what was wrong. It was just getting dark, and I figured maybe Dad was going home early. But when I got there, he still had the microphone in his hand.

"Ya gotta hear this," he said to me, and he took Paulie Romeo's transistor radio and put it up next to the microphone. The poker game had stopped, and I didn't know for sure what was going on until I heard Mel Allen's voice come out of the radio and through the PA system.

"The crowd here at Yankee Stadium is going crazy," he said. "After being on the disabled list for nearly two months, and after missing 61 games with a broken foot, Mickey Mantle is stepping in to pinch hit for the pitcher, Steve Hamilton. The Orioles have decided not to bring in a new pitcher, so lefthander George Brunet will face him, and Mickey will bat right-handed."

"Hey, what's going on?" Pete Montenaro said, when he came over to see why nobody was playing poker.

"Shad up," everybody told him. "Mantle's up at bat," and I noticed even more people were coming over, not to play poker, but to listen to the game.

"There's nobody on base, the Yankees are down by a run here in the seventh inning, and everybody in the place knows Mickey will be swinging for the fences."

"Don't do it, Mick," I told him, even though he was 180 miles away. "Keep your eye on the ball and just meet it. Don't try to kill it." He heard me, too; I'm sure of it.

"Mantle lets the first pitch go by for a strike."

"Good job, Mick," I said. "Don't want to be too anxious up there." Mel Allen kept talking, too, above the crowd noise.

"Yankee trainer, Gene Mauch, spoke to me between games and said if Mickey did pinch hit, he probably wouldn't be able to run hard, so if the Mick hits a ground ball to the infield, the Orioles will probably have an easy play at first base.

"Brunet winds again and fires. Mantle swings, and there's a drive deep to left field. I can't believe it. That ball is going . . . going . . . gone. A home run! Mickey Mantle has just tied this game up, and the crowd is going crazy."

The crowd at the poker booth was going crazy, too. Everybody was screaming and cheering. I ran over to the basketball booth to see if Larry and Bernie had heard. Bernie said that when they heard Mick hit the home run, Larry threw the basketball he was holding straight up in the air, and it almost hit Sister Patrick Francis when it came back down.

I ran back to the poker booth and was jumping up and down as I ran, just as if I'd hit the home run myself. Mel Allen was still describing the scene at the Stadium.

"Oh my," he said. "There's complete bedlam here. The score is tied at ten, and everybody's on their feet. The Oriole infielders are talking to Brunet near the mound, and the crowd is screaming for Mantle. And will you get a load of this? Jim Bouton and Joe Pepitone are actually pushing Mantle out of the dugout to take a bow. And there he is, tipping his hat to the crowd. The scene here, ladies and gentlemen, is electrifying. I've never heard or seen anything like it. This is truly unbelievable."

I couldn't believe it myself. "Thanks, Dad," I yelled before I went back to the baseball booth, and as the poker booth went back into action, too.

When I got back there, everybody was talking about Mickey's home run. And the kids throwing baseballs were so pumped up about it that they were throwing the balls as hard as they could and not hitting a thing. All I had to do was pick up the baseballs and toss them back to Coach Holland.

"I knew he was going to hit a home run," I told him, as I threw the balls back.

"Really?"

"Yeah. He promised me he wouldn't try to kill the ball the next time he got up."

I thought Coach Holland might ask me about my conversation with Mick, but Coach got talking to somebody else, so that was the end of that. Then, I heard a couple teenagers laughing about a rumor they had heard.

"Did you hear Angelo say that Mickey Mantle played baseball with them at the Cage last Thursday?" the first teenager said.

"Yeah, that's real believable," the other one answered sarcastically.

"Mickey Mantle was here in Amsterdam," I shouted. "He stayed in my house. He slept in my bed."

"Yeah, sure," the first one laughed again, as they walked away, and the second one yelled back, "Make sure you call me when the Mick comes again. Ha ha ha."

Big jerks. They don't believe anything unless they see it themselves.

"Last call for refreshments," Sister Susan shouted when she came by with her tray of goodies. I wanted to take a doughnut and throw it at the teenagers, but it was my favorite — a chocolate, cream-filled — so I ate it, instead. Then, I went back to setting up the wooden milk bottles and dreamed about our trip to Yankee Stadium later in the summer.

Mick didn't get back into the lineup full-time until the first week in September, and we didn't get down to the Stadium until after school had started again. Finally, on Saturday, September 7, Dad and I drove down the Thruway to New York, and we brought Bernie and Larry along with us. We were all so excited to actually be at Yankee Stadium that we were driving Dad nuts with our questions.

"What time is it, Mr. LaBate?"

"Where do we go in, Dad?"

"Can I buy an official Yankee cap?"

"Will you guys calm down, please? We got a half hour before the game starts. Mick said he'd leave tickets for us at the Main Gate, which is right over there. And, no, I don't want you to buy any souvenirs yet. Wait till we get inside."

While we waited for Dad to get the tickets, we overheard a couple guys talking about the small crowd for the game. "The Yanks are too good this year," one of them said. "They're in first place by 13 games, and there's only about 20 left."

"Yeah," the second one added. "I doubt if even 20,000 people will show up."

I didn't care how many people showed up as long as I finally got to see the inside of Yankee Stadium. I had seen so many games on television that I couldn't wait to see one in person. The outside of the Stadium looked just like I imagined it, only bigger. And I was fascinated by all the vendors outside selling hats, tee-shirts, pennants, buttons, photos, and small souvenir bats. Like Larry, I wanted to buy one of everything, even before we went inside.

When Dad finally came back with the tickets, we walked through the turnstiles and followed him as he led us through what looked like a big basement. We were surrounded by concrete walls. Once inside, we saw even more souvenir stands, and the vendors were really tempting us.

"Programs. Getcha programs here. You can't tell the players without a program. Getcha programs here."

"Yearbooks. Getcha yearbooks. Not many games left. Getcha yearbooks today."

"We're inside now, Mr. LaBate," Larry pleaded. "Can I buy a hat?"

"No, not yet. Let's go to our seats first."

"But my mom doesn't want me to get sunburn on my face."

Larry was really gettin' carried away now, and Dad saw right through him and laughed and played right along with him.

"Don't worry, Larry," he said. "If you start to get too red, we'll just leave early."

"No way!" Bernie yelled. "Let him burn. Who cares?"

We were all laughing, even Larry, when suddenly, Dad turned down a hallway, and the sunshine from the field hit us right in the face. Finally, I was seeing the ballfield at Yankee Stadium, and I couldn't believe my eyes. It looked just like the field at Mohawk Mills Park in Amsterdam when the grass is freshly cut, the chalk lines are down, and the flag is flying in center field.

How could that be? This is Yankee Stadium, home of the Bronx Bombers. How could the field itself look so much like Mohawk Mills Park? Maybe I dreamed so much about Yankee Stadium that I made it out to be more than it could be. Or maybe all fields really are the same. And maybe that's why Mickey had so much fun playing with us at the Cage.

I was stumbling behind everybody thinking about all these things when I realized we were getting closer and closer to the Yankee dugout. Dad had to show our tickets to the usher patrolling the seats closest to the field, and when we got to the first row of seats near the Yankee on-deck circle, the usher said, "Right here, gentlemen," and we each found a Yankee hat in our seat.

"Whoa!" Larry said. "Are these for us?" He didn't wait for an answer, though. He put the hat on and immediately bent the brim down on both edges.

"The Mick himself left those hats there for you," the usher told us, "so you guys must be pretty special."

Dad didn't look all that surprised, so he must have known, but Bernie looked like he was going to wet his pants. He put his hat on backward and started chattering as if he were behind the plate: "Hum babe, hum fire, hum chucker. Nothing but strikes, baby, nothing but strikes."

"Hey, down in front," somebody about five rows back yelled at all of us. We sat down immediately, and, as we did, the Yankees came running out for infield practice.

Just then, Mickey came out, too, and looked over to where we were sitting. I tried to call to him, but no words came out of my mouth. Even though I had no trouble talking to him a month earlier at our house, I was so flabbergasted to actually see him up close in his pinstriped uniform with his hat and glove that I could only wave to him. I couldn't say anything.

He walked over to the railing near our seats, and he really looked happy to see us. "Hi, Pete," he said to my dad as they shook hands. "Glad you made it. Everything go okay?"

"Well, our car didn't break down, if that's what you mean."

Mick laughed at that and said his car was running better than ever. "Your buddy Frank must really know what he's doing." Then, he reached out to shake our hands, too. "Hi, Jumbo. Hi, Larry. Hi, Barney."

When he got Bernie's name wrong, we all cracked up. "It's Bernie, not Barney," Larry corrected him.

"I know, I know," Mick laughed again, and then he was poking at us and gently slapping at us as if he wanted to take us all on. But when Larry reached over to grab his shirt, Mick danced away from the railing and said, "Gotta get back. Game's gonna start soon. I'll talk to you later." And he ran out to his position in center field.

I couldn't believe it. The managers were out near home plate exchanging the lineup cards. The Yankee infielders were making throws to Joe Pepitone at first base. Bob Sheppard was announcing the batting order to the crowd. And Mickey Mantle was fooling around with us like we were still at the Academy Street playground. The only thing that could have been better was if they let me and Larry play alongside Mick in the outfield and if they let Bernie put the equipment on to catch.

I stopped daydreaming when Larry poked me in the ribs and told me take off my hat for the National Anthem. During the song, however, I drifted off again as I looked around the Stadium. Mick was facing the flagpole way out near the monuments in center field, and I could see the number seven on the back of his uniform staring back at me.

I held my new Yankee cap over my heart like all the ballplayers on the field, and I looked hard at everything, so I'd never forget any of it: the umpires all gathered behind home plate; Stan Williams standing near the pitcher's mound, holding the game ball in his right hand, the resin bag lying nearby; all the fans standing at attention, some of them singing; and even the hot-dog and soda vendors were silent and not moving while Robert Merrill's voice echoed from the home-plate microphone out toward the fences in the outfield.

I couldn't get it all in. The National Anthem ended too soon, and the home-plate umpire shouted, "Play ball." The game was underway.

And as soon as we sat down, the usher who had shown us to our seats earlier brought over scorecards and hot dogs and sodas for all of us. "These are from Mick, too," he said. "Have a good time, and let me know if you need anything. Mick told me to take good care of you guys."

While eating my hot dog, I quick scribbled down the lineups, so I could keep score. Nobody did anything in the first inning, and the Tigers went ahead, one-nothing, with a run in the top of the second. As Mick prepared to lead off the second for the Yankees, he warmed up about 10 feet away from us. I tried to make eye contact with him, but he was all business. He swung three bats to get loose and watched left-hander Don Mossi warm up. Then, he stepped in to bat right-handed and promptly lined out to the shortstop. Once again, the whole thing happened too fast. I felt like I didn't even see it. Things slowed down after he hit, though, and the Yanks scored two runs to take a two-one lead.

With two outs in the bottom of the third, Mick came up again. This time, he looked at a few pitches and then drilled a hard single to left. Roger Maris and Elston Howard also followed with singles, and Mick came around to score. I thought for sure he would give us a smile or a laugh when he returned. I was wrong. He kept his head down as he shook hands with his teammates and disappeared into the dugout.

"Boy, is he serious!" Bernie said.

"What'd you expect?" Larry wisecracked. "Did you think he was going to stop here and ask us for batting tips?"

"Yes, as a matter of fact," I said to myself, without showing my disappointment.

In the fourth inning, the Tigers went crazy and scored five runs. First, Stan Williams gave up four singles and two runs. Then, when Ralph Houk replaced Williams with Steve Hamilton, he gave up another single and two more runs. The fifth run scored after Hector Lopez dropped an easy pop-fly in left field. We couldn't believe it.

"Boy, I coulda caught that one," I said confidently.

"I coulda caught that in my back pocket," Larry added, to emphasize that he was an even better fielder than I was.

"And I coulda caught it with my eyes closed," said Bernie, though we all knew that wasn't true.

"You guys are all dreamin'," Dad teased us. "You'd be shakin' in your shoes if you were out there."

"Would not," Larry said in self-defense.

"How 'bout that fly ball you dropped against Danny's Coffee House?" Bernie asked.

"That wasn't my fault. The sun was in my eyes."

While we were arguing, the Yankees finally got Detroit out, but the Tigers led 6-3. Larry and Bernie had both stopped keeping score by then, but I wanted to do the whole game. And I was glad I did. In the bottom of the fifth, the Yankees came back and broke the game wide open.

Mick started them off with another single, this time to center, and Roger Maris followed with a home run into the right-field stands. I really wanted to see Mick hit a home run, of course, but I have to admit that it was pretty exciting to see Roger hit one. When the two of them came back to the dugout together, they looked so great, walking side by side. The M and M boys. Maris and Mantle. I got chills just looking at them.

Next, Elston Howard doubled, Joe Pepitone singled, and Clete Boyer scored them both with a triple to deep center, and the Yankees led 7-6. The Tigers brought in a new pitcher who hit pinch-hitter Harry Bright, made an error on Bobby Richardson's bunt, and then gave up a single to Hector Lopez. The Yankees led 9-6, and, naturally, I expected Mick to hit a home run to top off the inning. He almost did, too. He brought all of us to our feet with a deep drive to center field, but there's just too much room out there. Billy Bruton raced out to the monuments and hauled it in by the 461 sign as Richardson and Lopez both tagged up and moved over. Then, Roger Maris came through with his second hit of the inning, a single to right for two more runs batted in and an 11-6 lead. A guy sitting behind us was listening to the game on the radio, and Mel Allen announced that the eight runs were the most the Yankees had scored in one inning all year.

"They couldn't have done it without us," Larry told the guy with the radio.

"Well, then, I'm glad you're here," he answered back.

Everybody stood to applaud the Yankees as they went back on the field for the top of the sixth, but we were disappointed, too. Instead of seeing number seven trot out to center field, we saw number 27, Jack Reed, go in to replace the Mick.

Once Mick was out of the game, though, we saw a lot more of him, and he was much more relaxed. Three or four times between innings, he came out of the dugout over to where we were sitting, and he talked to us about what was going on.

He said that whenever they had a big lead, Ralph Houk would take out one or two of the regular players to give them a rest and to give some of the substitutes and some of the younger players a chance to play. He said, too, that Houk did it even more late in the season, especially when it looked like they were going to win the pennant, and he wanted everybody well rested and healthy for the World Series.

"So can I play left field for Hector Lopez?" Larry asked. "He looks like he might be a little tired out there."

"I'll go get old Hector," Mick said, "so you can tell him that face to face."

Mick said it so seriously just before he returned to the dugout that Larry actually believed him and ran off to the restroom rather than face the possibility that "old Hector" might actually show up. He didn't, of course.

Nobody scored any runs in the last four innings, so it was pretty easy to keep score. Bernie kept hoping the Tigers would tie things up, so we could stay for extra innings, but it didn't happen. Those last few innings went quickly, too, because Mick made sure we had plenty of snacks to munch on: first, popcorn, then Cracker Jacks, and, finally, a giant ice-cream sandwich.

"I wish I could eat like this every day," I told Dad.

"I'll mention that to your mom when we get home," he laughed.

When the Yankees came out for the top of the ninth, Mick came over and whispered something to Dad, and Dad seemed to shake his head "Yes." I figured Mick was just asking if we were having a good time. Boy, was I wrong.

When relief pitcher Hal Reniff walked off the mound with the victory three outs later, we were all set to say good-by to Mick and head home. That's when he surprised us again. After congratulating his teammates on the victory, Mick came over to us and opened the gate near our seats.

"C'mon," he said. "Before you guys go back to Amsterdam, I'll show you the Clubhouse."

"I'm sorry, Mick. We really need to get going," Dad said, as serious as he could be. "We have a three-hour drive ahead of us."

I could tell he was kidding, of course, but Bernie and Larry weren't sure. Mick played along, too.

"Yeah, I guess you better hit the road then."

"Please, Mr. LaBate," Larry pleaded. "I'll wash your car for you when we get home. I promise."

"And I'll — I'll — I'll —"

Bernie was trying to come up with something even better to offer. We all waited for him to think of something.

"I'll do whatever you want me to do," he said finally. "I don't care what it is."

"All right, then," Dad gave in, and he winked at me. "I guess it's okay."

As we walked through the gate onto the grass near the dugout, Larry asked for one more thing. He tugged at Mick's uniform and said, "Mick, could we just walk on the field for one second? You know, inside the lines, so we can say we were actually on the field at Yankee Stadium?"

Mick saw that the grounds crew was already raking the basepaths, so he said, "Well, you can't run the bases or anything, but you can stand in the batter's box for a second if you want."

Larry ran over and stood near the plate as if he were hitting. We all followed him, and Mick started giving directions. "All right, Bernie, you catch. Jimbo, you get out there on the mound and I'll umpire."

Dad pulled out his camera and started snapping pictures. "Play ball!" Mick yelled. Then, he started announcing again, just like he did back at the Academy Street playground.

"It's the top of the ninth, ladies and gentlemen, the Yankees are ahead 3-2, but the Tigers have the bases loaded and their clean-up batter, Larry Borwhat, at the plate with a full count of three balls and two strikes. Jim LaBate is on the mound for the Yankees, and he looks to his catcher, Bernie Welch, for a signal."

I pretended to look in, and Bernie flashed his right index finger for a fastball. Then, I took a full windup and fired my best make-believe pitch. Mick announced the rest.

"LaBate winds and fires. Here comes the pitch. Borwhat swings and misses. Strike three. The game's over. The Yankees win."

Naturally, Larry didn't see it that way. When he took his imaginary swing, he saw a home run flying toward left, and while Mick was announcing the strikeout, Larry was announcing a different result.

"Borwhat hits it deep to left. That ball is going — going — gone! A home run!" He even started trotting toward first base, but Mick was on top of him in a second, and he picked him up and threw him over his shoulder. Larry tried to wiggle free. He didn't have a chance. Mick walked away like he was carrying a bag of garbage out toward the curb, and he didn't put Larry down until we got to the dugout. Mick kept announcing, too.

"That's Borwhat's fifth strikeout this game, ladies and gentlemen, so he's pretty upset, and the police are escorting him off the field. He'll probably be sent down to the minors tomorrow."

Dad was still taking pictures, and Bernie and I were laughing hysterically. We picked up all of our souvenirs before we entered the dugout and walked toward the hallway that led to the Clubhouse.

Roger Maris had just finished giving a post-game television interview, and he walked alongside. Mick introduced him to all of us, and Roger asked, "Which one of you guys struck out the great Mickey Mantle when he was up there visiting you?"

"I did," Larry bragged, immediately forgetting his make-believe adventure on the field. Mick put Larry down, so he could tell Roger his story, and we all walked down the ramp from the dugout to the Clubhouse, and the next thing I knew, we were surrounded by Yankees.

Most of them had their uniform shirts and spikes off already and were sitting around a buffet table in the center of the room eating sandwiches. A few reporters were talking to Hal Reniff about his pitching, but some of them left him as soon as Roger and Mick walked in. Before Mick answered any questions, though, he gave each one of us a baseball and a pen, and he told us we could get as many autographs as we wanted. He and Roger signed first.

Larry went looking for Whitey Ford, and Bernie went after Yogi. I really didn't want any other autographs since I already had the two best, but when Johnny Blanchard turned around and accidentally bumped into me, I didn't know what else to say but, "Can I have your autograph?"

He said, "Sure, son," and he signed "Big John — 38" in big letters. Then, I started asking for other autographs just so I'd have an excuse to talk to the other players. Most of them signed and went back to their sandwiches, but Bobby Richardson talked to me for about ten minutes. He asked me where I was from, what position I played, where I went to school, and where I went to church. When I told him all about St. Mary's, he told me how important it was to believe in Jesus and to give my life to Him. He really surprised me because I'd never heard anybody but a priest or a nun talk that way. He was so gentle and soft-spoken, too. I could hardly believe I was talking to the Most Valuable Player of the 1960 World Series. He was my second favorite ballplayer from that day on.

After about a half hour, and after getting just about everybody's autograph, Dad said it was time to go. So, we went over to Mick's locker and thanked him again for everything. He shook our hands, he had Tom Tresh use Dad's camera to take a picture of all of us together, and then he walked us to the exit, and said good-by. Our day with the Mick was finally over.

In the World Series that year, the Yankees got swept by the Dodgers in four straight games. Mick went two for 15, with one big home run off Sandy Koufax and five strikeouts. The Yankees never won a World Series again while Mick played.

In the 1964 World Series, Mick hit three home-runs against the Cardinals, but the Yankees lost in seven games. I remember I was delivering newspapers on the top of McDougal Street and listening to my transistor radio as Bob Gibson struck out Clete Boyer for the final out.

During Mick's last four years, the Yankees were never even close to winning the pennant, and his batting average and his home-run totals dropped significantly. He still made the All-Star team every year, of course, but usually all he did was strike out and then get a standing ovation.

By the time he retired at the beginning of the 1969 season, I realized my baseball career was coming to an end, too. I was good enough to play in the Rookie League, and I was good enough to play on the Junior Varsity and Varsity teams at St. Mary's, but I wasn't good enough to play after that.

I played my last high-school game on Friday, June 7, and the Yankees retired Mickey's number seven the next day at Yankee Stadium.

Dad and I had great seats again that day, but with Mick's family there and all his friends and old teammates there, too, Mick only had a second or two to come over and say "Hello." That's why whenever I hear anybody talk about Mickey Mantle and the special day he had at the end of his career, I tell them all about the most special day of all — Mickey Mantle Day in Amsterdam.

The End

Mickey Mantle
1931-1995

Epilogue

Bobby Richardson's Homily for Mickey Mantle on August 15, 1995

A father had a dream, and that dream became a reality when Mutt Mantle saw his son play in the Major Leagues. And we're here today to grieve the loss of one who was much loved: a husband, a father, a grandfather — Mallory calls him "Pa Pa Mickey" — a brother, an uncle, a friend, and to all of us, a baseball legend. Merlyn, Mickey, Jr., David, and Danny, God bless you, as you have shown your love and care these last days like I've not witnessed before.

First Thessalonians, the fourth chapter, the 13th verse through the 18th, offers comfort at a time like this: "But I would not have you to be ignorant, brethren, concerning them which are asleep, that ye sorrow not, even as others which have no hope. For if we believe that Jesus died and rose again, even so them also which sleep in Jesus will God bring with him. For this we say unto you by the word of the Lord, that we which are alive and remain unto the coming of the Lord shall not prevent them which are asleep. For the Lord himself shall descend from heaven with a shout, with the voice of the archangel, and with the trump of God: and the dead in Christ shall rise first: Then we which are alive and remain shall be caught up together with them in the clouds, to meet the Lord in the air: and so shall we ever be with the Lord. Wherefore comfort one another with these words" (King James Version). Let's pray.

Father, as we've listened to the story of Mickey's life and death being broadcast all over the nation, we're reminded of the words of Moses from Psalm 90: "We spend our days as a tale that is told (Verse 9)." And we know that one day, we will all stand before you as our Creator. We're just so thankful that you provided a way, the Lord Jesus Christ, who suffered and died for our sins on the cross, so that we might have everlasting life with you. We ask your blessing on this service and your blessing on the family. Be a comfort to them and meet each one here today at their point of need. We pray in Jesus' name. Amen.

Mickey Mantle was the kind of ballplayer, the kind of person that people were attracted to, and so while we grieve, we also honor Mickey, as we remember his life and the special ways and memories that touched us all.

I want to make a transition now from crying and sadness to laughter because if you know Mickey, he was always laughing. And he enjoyed playing football in the backyard with the boys. He enjoyed golf games at Preston Trails with the boys and their traveling to autograph sessions with him. But the teammates who are here today also know that he always kept all of us laughing.

I remember the mongoose in Detroit in the clubhouse. I remember the snake he put in Marshall Bridges' uniform in Kansas City before he was dressing that day. Mickey always ran out of money, and he borrowed money from Yogi, and Yogi would charge him 50% — no, that's not in there. Take that back, Yogi.

Yogi flew in today on Bob Hope's plane, and he's flying out tomorrow with President Ford's plane. But Yogi was the manager in 1964. The Yankees lost four games in a row in Chicago. Tony Kubek had bought some harmonicas. He gave one to Phil Linz. Phil didn't play in any of those ballgames, but on the bus, with Yogi in the front, he chose this time to learn how to play his harmonica. Well, he played for a while, and Yogi took as much as he could, and, finally, he jumped up and he said, "Put that thing in your pocket."

He didn't use those words, but something to that effect. And Phil was in the back of the bus, and he didn't hear what Yogi said, and asked, "What'd he say?"

Mickey was sitting over across the aisle, and he whispered back: "He said he couldn't hear you. Play it again."

And Yogi was the manager in '64 when Whitey Ford and Mickey started talking about how good they were in other sports, basketball in particular. And it ended up that when we played the Cadets at West Point, Whitey was to have the pitchers and catchers, and Mickey was to have the infielders and outfielders, and there would be a great game at the gymnasium at West Point after the regulars got out of the lineup. Well, Yogi said, "Somebody's gonna get hurt."

Well, Mickey did it right. He had uniforms for his players, he had a limousine, he had a chauffeur, and they took the players from Mickey's team over to the game and came back. And it was a great game. Mickey's team won. Tommy Tresh was voted most valuable. Yogi was right. Steve Hamilton, the only one who played professional basketball, turned his ankle, and he was hurt.

But you know, there are so many good things that Mickey did that people never heard about. I remember he flew across the country for Fritz Bickell when he was dying with cancer. In this church (Lovers Lane United Methodist Church in Dallas), right here, he did a benefit for a Missions Outreach. And over the years, he very seldom said "No."

He came to my hometown on numerous occasions, but in particular for the YMCA. We had a great banquet, there was a highlights film, and then we went out to the ballpark, and Mickey was to give a batting exhibition, something that you just can't imagine him doing. Tony Kubek was there. Tony throws straight overhanded, same speed all the time, and he was chosen to pitch to Mickey. Everything was all set, but Tony changed up on Mickey on the first pitch, and he swung and missed and pulled his leg, and if he could have run, he would have chased Tony around the outfield. Tony made up for it, though; he hit one in the light towers in right field in the Oldtimer's Game that followed.

But underneath all of Mickey's laughter and kindness, there was a fear of death and an emptiness that he tried to cover and fill, sometimes with harmful choices. Remember, Bob (Costas), when he said on your interview, "There's still an emptiness inside"?

The last game that Mickey and I played together was October the second, 1966. It was in Chicago, and we were at the Bismark Hotel, and I had invited a friend, a friend of mine and a friend of Mickey's, to come over and speak to the ballclub. His name was Billy Zeoli, president of Gospel Films. I remember standing in the back of the room that was set aside, and most of the players were there in attendance. And I was looking over their shoulders at the fine, efficient, professional baseball players who were there. And yet I knew that all of us had problems. Some financial, some marital, problems of various natures. And yet my friend that day gave the answer to each one of these problems in the person of Jesus Christ.

He held his Bible up, and he said, "The Bible says three things. Number one, the Bible says there's a problem, and the problem is sin.

"Number two, the Bible gives the answer to the problem in the person of Jesus Christ.

"And number three, the Bible demands a decision." And then he turned around, and he had a blackboard and a piece of chalk, and he wrote this question up on the blackboard: "What have you done with Jesus Christ?"

And then he went on to give three possible answers. Number one, to say "Yes," to accept Jesus Christ as Lord and Savior. And I remember looking around that room at some of my teammates who I knew had said "Yes" to Christ.

The second possibility was to say "No." And I knew there were some of us who were unwilling to give up, perhaps, what we had going at that time.

And the third possibility was to say "Maybe," to put it off to a more convenient time with good intentions. But my friend made this statement. He said, "Saying 'maybe,' because of the X factor of death, automatically puts you in the 'No' category."

I didn't really understand that then, but some years later, not too many years ago, we had a reunion of the 1961 New York Yankees in Atlantic City, New Jersey. The players were there in attendance. It was a wonderful time of thinking back and remembering. But in my room that night, I realized that three were not there: Roger Maris, who broke Babe Ruth's home-run record, in a battle with cancer; Elston Howard, that fine catcher on the ballclub, with a heart condition; and a young pitcher by the name of Duke Maas.

And so I understood what he meant when he said, "Because of the X factor of death, it's really 'No.'" So there are really only two choices: one, to say "Yes"; the other "No."

And, then, my big thrill in baseball occurred, when a young teammate of mine, who played for the next seven or eight years, came up, and said, "You know, I've never heard that before — a personal relationship with a living Savior who gives to us an abundant life. I would like to receive Jesus Christ as my Savior."

And that's the excitement, but there's more excitement. I came here to Dallas during the All-Star break this past month. Mickey Mantle and Whitey Ford and I serve on the Bat Board, and I was here because of that. And I had gotten the number from Whitey, and I called Mickey, and we had a great conversation together.

And, then, the next morning, about six o'clock, he called my room, and Betsy answered the phone, and he said, "Betsy, is Bobby there? I'd like for him to pray for me. And we had a wonderful time on the telephone that morning praying, and I remember that I used this verse of Scripture. I said, "Mickey, there's a great verse in Philippians 4. It says, 'Delight yourself in the Lord. Find your joy in him at all times. Never forget his nearness.' And then it says, 'Tell God in details, your problems, your anxieties, and the promise is the peace of God, which passeth all understanding, shall keep our hearts and minds as we rest in Christ Jesus'" (Verses 6-7).

We talked two or three more times, and I went on back to South Carolina, and I received a call from Roy True, his friend and lawyer, and he said "Mickey's not doing very well, and the family would like for you to consider the possibility of coming out and being in the service."

And I asked Merlyn if it would be all right if I could come on out, and she said "Yes."

Well, I came in on, I guess it was last Wednesday night. Friends picked me up at the airport, and I spent the night with them; it was late. And the next morning, I drove over to Baylor Hospital. Whitey Ford was just walking out at the time, and Mickey had really perked up with Whitey's visit. And as I walked in and went over to his bed, he had that smile on his face, and he looked at me, and the first thing he said was, "Bobby, I've been wanting to tell you something. I want you to know that I've received Christ as my Savior."

Well, I cried a little bit, I'm sure, and we had prayer together, and then in a very simple way, I said, "Mickey, I just want to make sure." And I went over God's plan of Salvation with him: That God loved us and had a plan and purpose for our life, and sent His Son, the Lord Jesus Christ, to shed His precious blood, and promised in His Word that if we would repent of our sins and receive the Lord Jesus, that we might not only have everlasting life, but also the joy of letting Him live His life in us.

Mickey said, "That's what I've done."

Well, the big three came in that afternoon: that's Moose Skowron and Hank Bauer and Johnny Blanchard, and they had a wonderful visit again with Mickey. My wife and I came back later that afternoon, and I remember that Mickey was in bed, but he wanted to be in the reclining chair, and David and Danny and a couple of the others, I think, helped him over. He was laughing then when David grabbed him. Mickey said, "Do you want to dance?"

But he sat in the chair, and my wife, Betsy, sat down by him and shared her testimony. And then she asked him a question. She said, "Mickey, if God were here today, and if you were standing before Him, and He would ask you the question, 'Why should I let you in my heaven?' what would you say?"

And quick as a flash, he said. "For God so loved the world, that He gave His only begotten Son, that whosoever believeth in Him should not perish but have everlasting life" (John 3:16).

Well, I guess it was a little bit later, and I said, "Mickey, do you remember your day in New York? You had heard me use a little poem called 'God's Hall of Fame.' You talked about using it that day."

He said, "Yeah, I should have."

I said, "No, I'm not sure that was the right time, Mickey."

But ya know, I think it is the right time today. It says it all. It says:

"Your name may not appear down here in this world's Hall of Fame.
In fact, you may be so unknown that no one knows your name.
The trophies, the honors, the flashbulbs here may pass you by and neon lights of blue.
But if you love and serve the Lord, then I have news for you.
This Hall of Fame is only good as long as time shall be.
But keep in mind God's Hall of Fame is for eternity.
This crowd on Earth may soon forget the heroes of the past.

They cheer like mad until you fall, and that's how long you last.
But in God's Hall of Fame,
by just believing in His Son, inscribed you'll find your name.
I tell you, friend, I wouldn't trade my name, however small,
that's written there beyond the stars in that Celestial Hall.
For every famous name on Earth or glory that they share.
I'd rather be an unknown and have my name up there."

At Mickey's last press conference, he once again mentions his struggle with alcohol and a desire to be a dad to his boys. He also mentioned his real heroes, the organ donors. I hope you will all support the Mickey Mantle Foundation that addresses these issues and join his team.

But if Mick could hold a press conference from where he is today, I know that he would introduce you to his true hero, the One who died in his place to give him not just a longer physical life, but everlasting life: his Savior, Jesus Christ.

And the greatest tribute that you could give Mickey today will be for you to receive his Savior, too. Let's bow for prayer.

Thank you, God, that You loved us so much that You gave Your only Son who willingly came and died for our sins, according to the Scriptures, and that He was buried and rose again the third day, according to the Scriptures. May each of us today honestly answer the question, "What have I done with Jesus?"

I'm so glad that someone shared with me years ago, and, perhaps, you'd like to pray now as I did then: "God, thank You for loving me and sending your Son to shed His precious blood, and right now, I'm sorry for my sin, and I receive You as Lord and Savior. Thank You for coming into my heart. To God be the glory."

The Author . . .

Jim LaBate grew up in Amsterdam, New York, and graduated from Saint Mary's Institute and Bishop Scully High School. He earned a bachelor's degree in English from Siena College in Loudonville, New York, and a master's degree in English from the College of Saint Rose in Albany, New York.

Jim served as a Peace Corps Volunteer in Costa Rica for two years, taught high-school English for ten years (one year at Vincentian Institute in Albany, New York, and nine years at Keveny Memorial Academy in Cohoes, New York), and worked as a writer at Newkirk Products, Inc., in Albany, New York, for ten years.

He currently teaches writing courses at Hudson Valley Community College in Troy, New York, in addition to his writing activities.

Jim lives in Clifton Park, New York, with his wife, Barbara, and their two daughters: Maria and Katrina.

Let's Go, Gaels

Let's Go Gaels — a novella by Jim LaBate — tells the story of one week in the life of a 12-year-old boy.

The story takes place in a Catholic school in upstate New York in 1964. As the week begins, the narrator is thinking about a speech he has to give in English class on Friday, a big basketball game on Saturday, and a trip to the movies on Saturday night.

During the week, however, something happens that changes his life — and his outlook on life — forever. The event moves him further away from his innocent boyhood and closer to his eventual maturity as a man.

Order Form

Please send to the following address:

Name ______________________________

Address ______________________________

City ____________________ State ________ Zip ________

Let's Go, Gaels	$5.95 × _____	copies =	______
Mickey Mantle Day in Amsterdam	$7.95 × _____	copies =	______
Postage	$1.25 × _____	copies =	______
		Subtotal	______
New York residents add appropriate sales tax			______
		Total	______

Please enclose a check for your order and mail to:

Mohawk River Press

Mohawk River Press
P.O. Box 4095
Clifton Park, New York 12065-0850